I0588491

SHAMUS AND ANTHONY COMMIT CAPERS

TEN TALES OF CRIMINALS, CROOKS, AND CULPRITS

SHAMUS AND ANTHONY COMMIT CAPERS

TEN TALES OF CRIMINALS, CROOKS, AND CULPRITS

EDITED BY

GAY TOLTL KINMAN & ANDREW MCALEER

LEVEL

SHORT

First published by Level Short 2024

Copyright © 2024 by Gay Toltl Kinman & Andrew McAleer, Editors

All rights reserved. No part of this publication may be reproduced, stored or transmitted in any form or by any means, electronic, mechanical, photocopying, recording, scanning, or otherwise without written permission from the publisher. It is illegal to copy this book, post it to a website, or distribute it by any other means without permission.

Gay Toltl Kinman & Andrew McAleer, Editors, assert the moral right to be identified as the authors of this work.

This book is entirely a work of fiction. The names, characters and incidents portrayed in it are the work of the authors' imaginations. Any resemblance to actual persons, living or dead, events or localities is entirely coincidental.

Original stories copyrighted by their individual authors.

First edition

ISBN: 978-1-68512-788-6

Cover art by Level Best Designs

This book was professionally typeset on Reedsy.
Find out more at reedsy.com

Contents

Praise for Kinman & McAleer's Awards Winner Mystery Series

Praise for *Shamus & Anthony Commit Capers*

"Andrew McAleer's and Gay Totl Kinman's latest crime fiction anthology, *Shamus & Anthony Commit Capers*, is a superb collection of thrilling suspense stories structured around the art of the con. Authentic and brilliantly plotted stories by some of today's hottest and most wanted swindlers, grifters, and hustlers…I mean mystery writers!"—Kris Meyer, Executive Producer, Super Troopers 2

"Enter the thrilling world of *Shamus & Anthony Commit Capers*, where crime and unforgettable characters collide in original tales by ten maestros of mystery mayhem. From harebrained bank jobs to schemes gone wild, buckle up for a rollercoaster ride of wit, twists, and camaraderie. With every turn, expect the unexpected. Because in this underworld anything goes—and usually does. A riotous read for mystery fans."—BV Lawson, Derringer Award winner and author of the Shamus Award finalist Scott Drayco mystery series

"Even the best-laid plans can go wrong, and that's what happens to the bungling criminals in this masterful collection of ten calamitous capers."—Michael Bracken, Anthony, Edgar, and Shamus nominee

Praise for *Edgar and Shamus Go Golden*

"Sit back with *Edgar and Shamus Go Golden* and savor original mystery tales written exclusively by Edgar Allan Poe and Shamus Award-winning authors. In something of a coup Edgar winner John McAleer's 'Case of the Illustrious Banker' makes its debut, more than 80 years since it was written."—Crime Fiction Lover

"*Edgar and Shamus Go Golden* is a 24-carat collection of stories by the best in the business, proving that we are in a new Golden Age ourselves, and lucky to be here."—SJ Rozan, Edgar Award winner and bestselling author of *Family Business*

"*Edgar and Shamus Go Golden* is a must-read. Editors Gay Toltl Kinman and Andrew McAleer assembled a collection of stories that fit together like the songs on a Beatles album, with one story setting up the next. Each piece captures the Golden Age glow the editors promised. I highly recommend it."—Tom MacDonald, Shamus Award finalist of the Dermot Sparhawk P.I. series

"As if picking up where Sir Arthur Conan Doyle, Dame Agatha Christie, and Dorothy Sayers left off, the who-dun-it, why-dun-it, how-dun-it, and unshakable alibi are all afoot in Edgar and Shamus. Travel back in time with an all-star cast of some of today's leading experts in the art of crime fiction."—The Big Thrill

"The Golden Age of Mystery will continue for as long as writers produce stories that challenge us to find solutions alongside the detectives. These stories in *Edgar and Shamus Go Golden*—some of the best of the best—offer definitive proof."—Stephen D. Rogers, Derringer Award-winning author of *Shot to Death*

"[A] fine introduction to a couple of characters I'd love to see again."—Thrilling Detective Website on Carolina Garcia-Aguilera's Shamus nominated "The Pearl of Antilles" in *Edgar & Shamus Go Golden*

"John McAleer's 'Case of the Illustrious Banker'...is just one of the treasures unearthed...in *Edgar & Shamus Go Golden*."—Midwest Book Review

Introduction

By Stephen D. Rogers

In the crime fiction genre a caper is a story that focuses on a crime, generally non-violent, and typically a theft. The perpetrators often aren't the masterminds that you would find in a heist movie, but tend to be average people, perhaps less than average, perhaps even bumblers.

While criminals trying to pull off a caper might synchronize their watches ("You didn't tell me I needed to bring a watch.") or build scale models ("I couldn't find the blueprints for the bank we're going to rob, and so I based this diorama on a memory of a bank I once saw in a movie."), they're just as likely to start the job with a heartfelt, "What could go wrong?"

Therein lies the power of the form: "What could go wrong?"

We relish the exploits undertaken in a caper because we see can ourselves in the everyday protagonists, actively pursuing their dreams. After all, it is the optimism behind the question "What could go wrong?" that allows us to navigate our own lives and a changing world.

A caper encourages giddy self-confidence, emphasizes the importance of taking risks, and offers hope that things can get better—that things will get better—once the job is complete.

As such, a caper is the antithesis of noir, where everything can and will go wrong, where the protagonist is doomed to failure or even death. In a caper, even if things don't go according to plan, and nothing ever goes according to plan, the protagonists will at least be rewarded with the knowledge that they had the courage to try.

And next time? An adjustment here, an adjustment there. Next time will be different. Next time, we're going to get away clean with the treasure intact. After all, what could go wrong?

Please enjoy this assembly of *Shamus & Anthony Commit Capers* stories by some of the best in the business, stories that range from dark to light, stories that remind us what it means to be human. Read, and then emerge transformed.

Stephen D. Rogers,
Buzzard's Bay, Massachusetts

Scamming the Scammer

By Marcia Muller

"I lost my life savings to that scammer. Thirty thousand dollars. Everything I had," Ana Emery told me.

"This was an internet scam?" I asked.

"No, Ms. McCone. I don't have a computer, don't much like them. It happened on the phone."

I frowned. Internet scammers are fairly easy to trace; I have an employee at my agency—Derek Frye—who can identify one with a few strokes of his keyboard. But phone scammers are not as simple: they change their number often, re-route their calls deviously, assume identities with the artistry of Academy Award-winning actors.

"Tell me how it happened," I said.

She fiddled with the edge of her Irish-knit sweater, uncrossed and recrossed her legs.

Ashamed of her foolishness, I thought.

My new client struck me as someone who was very concerned with projecting a confident image as an executive assistant in one of San Francisco's high-powered law firms. She'd been referred to me by her boss, my old friend criminal defense attorney Glenn Solomon, who'd called her—in retro-speak manner—"one sharp cookie." But the cookie appeared to be crumbling now as she sat across my desk from me in one of the clients' chairs. She looked around the office at everything but me.

"Ms. Emery?" I prompted.

She roused herself and sighed. "I just feel so stupid."

"No need for that. Thousands of people are scammed every day. Why don't you start at the beginning?"

She sighed again, ran her fingers through her short, feather-cut hair. It was almost as black as my own, except for feint reddish highlights. "This woman called. I don't normally pick up the phone unless I know who's calling, but I was cooking and expecting to hear from my friend Janey, so I did. She said, 'Hi, this is Daniela.' Now, I *do* have a friend called Daniela, but I was surprised to hear from her since she lives in Paris. So surprised that I said, 'Hey, what's happening?' We chatted; she asked me about my job and my new car and recommended a few investment opportunities, which I decided to take her up on."

"And when did you act on that decision?"

"The very next morning. They sounded too good to pass up."

"Let me guess: these opportunities involved cryptocurrency."

"Yes. I wish I'd never heard that term."

I know a good amount about cryptocurrency. It's been around a few years now, to very mixed reviews. Hailed as the new wave of high-earning investment, it is purely digital, bypassing banks and other financial institutions, and since its inception has been plagued by serious drawbacks. Purchases in such currencies as Bitcoin, Etherium, Litcoin and SafeTcoin are uninsured, hard to convert, and subject to extreme volatility. Huge price swings can wipe out fortunes in nanoseconds.

"Which crypto exchange did you have your account with?"

"SafeTcoin. Daniela recommended it."

SafeTcoin was the least reliable of all the exchanges.

"Did you talk with Glenn before you invested?"

"No. I wanted to, but he's been involved in a high-profile murder trial, and I didn't feel I should bother him. Plus, I wanted to prove I could do something on my own."

Pride goeth before, I thought.

"When did you realize your funds had been wiped out?" I asked

"The second day after I transferred them in. I called Daniela's number in Paris. And then I knew."

"It wasn't Daniela you'd been speaking with."

"As soon as she answered, I knew it hadn't been her voice on the phone. The voice had been close but a little off."

I'd expected this. "What information did you share with the fake Daniela?"

"Everything. She said she needed it to help set up a wallet—one of those digital things where they store your information—for me."

"Even your social security number?"

She nodded. "I know they say you should never give it out, but Daniela—the real one—has been my friend forever. I felt safe with her."

I hesitated, doodling on the legal pad where I'd been taking notes. "Okay," I said, "I'll need one of my staff to get in touch with Daniela in Paris so he can get a voiceprint on her. Also copies of your savings and investment statements and any communications with the fraud departments you contacted. And anything else you may feel is pertinent to the investigation."

She nodded and stood up, clearly relieved the interview was at an end.

After she was gone, I moved from the desk to one of the sofas in the conversation area of my office. Stared out at the flurries of late February rain that washed the plate glass window. Thought about how I'd pursue this new investigation. Before I left to go home to my house in the Marina district—and to my husband Hy's great chicken cacciatore—I made a list of additional questions to ask Ana Emery.

* * *

The morning was as gloomy as the day before. I drove my Miata to the McCone & Ripinsky Building in the financial district, parked in the underground garage, and took the elevator to the top floor. Ana Emery was already there, a typed list of the answers to my questions and a sheaf of documents in hand. I poured coffee from the carafe on the table and seated Ana in the conversation area, where—as I'd supposed—she seemed more at ease than in the formal setting across my desk. While we sipped, I glanced over the list. No surprises there; I'd turn it over to Derek for fact-checking.

After a moment I said to Ana, "The voiceprint from Daniela came in last night. I didn't think it could possibly be a match. As you probably realize most scammers don't know their victims, which makes them so hard to trace. But from what you've told me, this woman seemed to have a lot of your personal information. I think we need to take a look at your other women friends."

"Oh, I don't believe any of them could be responsible…"

"It's still a possibility. Who are they?"

"Well, I…I don't actually have many. I'm not what you'd call gregarious. There's Janey Woodman, who I was expecting a call from when I first heard from the fake Daniela. Lee Leveroni. Becca Sissel. That's about it."

"Are they work friends?"

"No. I went to high school with Becca. Lee I met at a book group about three years ago. It bored me, so I quit. Janey used to live in my old building on Arguello; we've kept in touch."

I wrote down the names and contact information, then asked, "Any male friends?"

"No." She colored slightly. "I used to date a guy named Mark Evans, but he moved to Silicon Valley a few months ago. Besides, aren't you looking for a woman?"

"Or a man who put her up to this scam."

She pressed her fingertips to her lips. "I hadn't thought of that."

It seemed to me there were a lot of things she hadn't thought of.

"Besides," she added, "Mark doesn't need money. He's independently wealthy."

"To some people, any amount of wealth isn't enough." I made a check mark beside the next item on my list. "Okay, Ms. Lewis, what do you do for fun?"

"Fun?" She made it sound like a foreign term.

"Do you play sports? Take classes? Take photographs or paint or travel? You mentioned a book group—anything else like that?"

"Why do you need to know those things?"

"Just trying to get a picture of your life."

"Oh. Well, I *did* take a cooking class at Le Ecole a while back, but it didn't work out so well. Turns out I've got no talent as a cook."

"What about going to nightclubs?"

"I don't drink."

"Not even to listen to music? Or dance?"

"Well, I went once to Jude's Tavern—that place on Van Ness—with Janey, but I hated it. It was crowded and hot, and the music was loud. I never went back."

I wanted to snap, "Is there anything you do *do*?" but I held back. The client, I always proclaim to my employees, must always be coddled and cosseted.

* * *

"Your administrative assistant," I told Glenn, "is a real nothing woman."

We were seated over drinks in Rosanna's, on the 31st floor of Embarcadero Three, his favorite after-work venue. The rain had worsened, slashing at the windows, and neither of us had cared to venture out.

"I said she was a smart cookie, not Miss Personality."

"More appropriately—in your vernacular—Miss Wet Blanket."

"Give the girl a break."

"I'm trying to. But what the hell is wrong with her?"

"Difficult childhood."

"How so?"

He frowned, ran his fingers through his thick white hair. "Her father left the family when Ana was ten. Went to live with a friend of her mother's down the street from them and later divorced the mother and married the new woman. The mother became an alcoholic and died of an overdose of sleeping pills three years later. The father took Ana in, but his new wife treated her badly. Ana left at sixteen—underage, but her father didn't try to stop her."

"And after that?"

"Surprisingly, Ana pulled herself together. Moved in with a friend's family and exchanged babysitting services for her room and board. Graduated high school early and attended paralegal classes while holding what she calls 'a string of nothing jobs.' Came to me two, two and a half years ago. She's been an excellent employee."

"I see she gave her address as a studio apartment south of Market, not too far from the M&R building."

"Singles place. She could have afforded better before this scam occurred, but she said she was saving to buy a house."

"She's still there?"

"Rent is paid up until the end of the month?"

"And then?"

Glenn looked embarrassed, as he always does when caught in a kindness. "I'll cover it until this mess is cleaned up."

"I notice none of the three friends whose names she gave to me live at that address. I'd have thought she'd connect with more people in a singles place."

"Friends don't seem to be big on her agenda."

"Nothing else does, either."

"McCone, you seem to have taken a dislike to Ana."

"Not a dislike. It's just that passionless people irritate me."

He considered that. "Come to think of it, me too."

* * *

I spent a couple of hours setting up appointments to interview Ana's three friends: Janey Woodman, Lee Leveroni, and Becca Sissel. Before I'd called the women I'd listened to the voiceprint of the real Daniela: the register was low, but strong, with a silent French accent. The women's voices were all low and strong, but none had an accent. Of course, accents can easily be faked.

Becca worked at home in interior design. Her office was in a spacious condo on Scott Street, crowded with three drawing boards for her assistants. She took me into a glassed-in conference room and gave me coffee. From her surroundings I assumed she was affluent and worked hard at it—I doubted she had the need or the time to pull off a complicated scam.

She seemed genuinely concerned about Ana's problem. "I wish she'd let

6

me know. I could easily have helped tide her over. Is there any way she can recover the money?"

"It's doubtful. Scams like this—especially ones involving cryptocurrency—are designed to move funds very quickly. What I'm primarily concerned with now is to prevent any more losses, and we're monitoring her few existing accounts—like credit cards—on an hourly basis. She provided information to the scammer that might make it possible for her to tap into whatever little remains."

"I'm going to phone her, see if there's anything I can do."

"I'm sure she'll appreciate that."

* * *

Ana didn't; she called me shortly before I left for home, railing at my invading her privacy. "I brought this problem to you because Glenn stressed your high value on confidentiality!"

"The women you named are your friends.

"They won't be if they find out what a fool I've been."

"Becca sounded as if she was anxious to help."

"Anxious to look down her nose at me! She's already wired five thousand dollars into my bank account, as if I were some poor relation."

"I'd say that was a very kind gesture."

"The hell it was! You don't know Becca."

"I guess not. Ana, do you want me to go on with this inquiry?" I'd have been delighted if she'd said no.

But instead, she said grudgingly, "Yes, of course—go ahead."

Damn! I told her I'd be in touch.

* * *

I met Janey Woodman the next morning at a coffee shop on Haight Street. The neighborhood—long ago known as the birthplace of the hippie movement—has undergone various changes over the past few decades and is now gentrified. The coffee shop was shiny with chrome and plush with leather, an oasis from the rain that still pelted the city.

Janey Woodman, who lived upstairs from the shop and clerked at a nearby bed-and-bath store, reminded me of the quintessential earth mother: long brown hair gathered at the nape of her neck; no makeup; plain shapeless clothing. Her earrings were clusters of some kind of seed and matched a double strand around her neck. She ordered a cinnamon latte while I opted for black coffee.

"Ana and I went to parochial school together—Saint Mary's," she told me. "Actually, we lived together the last two years after she moved out on her father and new stepmother. She traded babysitting services with my folks in exchange for room and board."

"So you've been close a long time."

She frowned. "Not close, actually. Ana doesn't get close to anybody. Never has. But we've kept in touch. I've tried to be a friend, and the past couple of years, I've concentrated on breaking her out of her shell—getting her to do stuff like take classes, go to concerts, go clubbing. I haven't been real successful."

"She mentioned not liking Jude's Tavern very much."

"She *hated* it. Even though she met Mark Evans there."

The boyfriend who moved to Silicon Valley. "That was a serious relation-ship?"

"He wanted it to be, asked her to marry him and move to Santa Clara. She refused. He still comes up to the city, and I see him around Jude's Tavern now and then. He always asks about her."

I'd try to contact Mark Evans later.

"Anything else you could tell me about Ana?" I asked.

Janey considered, spooning up the last of her latte. "Not really. I've given her gifts from the store where I work, even offered her a place to stay till she gets on her feet. But to tell the truth, I've soured on the friendship. You go out of your way to try to help somebody, and they don't appreciate it—that's kind of a losing situation, isn't it?"

* * *

So Becca Sissel had helped to the extent of five thousand dollars. Janey Woodman hadn't been successful in bringing her out of her shell and was cooling on the friendship. Had Lee Leveroni been similarly repulsed? I'd have to ask her, but Lee was a flight attendant and I couldn't meet with her until after her four o'clock return on Southwest. I hadn't visited my office in the M&R building yet that day, so I stopped there and spent a few hours going over the numerous operatives' reports that were clogging my in box.

Missing persons: two of them, no progress. Easy to get lost in this city. Check forgery, but the family didn't want the police involved, just wanted to confront the cheating son and probably beat the hell out of him. Petty thefts from a small clothing store; owner merely wanted photographs of the light-fingered employee. Missing grandchildren of legal age. Threatening calls in the Sunset district, probably from a neighbor. Car vandalism. Missing electric bike. Graffiti on sidewalk. Surveillance on Pickleball courts as a possible basis for a nuisance suit. Missing Pickleball paddles....

Finally, it was time to meet Lee Leveroni at her apartment on Russian Hill. It was in a small wood-shingled building sandwiched between two nondescript highrises that must have provided good views of the Bay. Lee—blonde, well-groomed—had changed from her airline uniform to blue sweats and seemed to be glad to be at home. She offered me a glass of wine—which I gratefully accepted—and seated me on a black sofa whose fabric was shot with gold threads.

"So Ana's up to her old tricks," she said.

"I'm not sure what you mean by that."

"Poor mouthing."

"She's been the victim of a scam—"

"Ana is a perpetual victim."

"Her entire assets have been wiped out in a cryptocurrency confidence scheme."

"What assets?"

"Stocks, bonds, pension fund, bank accounts."

Lee Leveroni looked surprised. "I didn't think she was so prudent with her money. I've never known her to save. Ana spends and spends. Always has. Always will."

* * *

Somebody was lying to me.

Lee Leveroni? She was a distant friend from a book club she and Ana had once attended. I'd questioned her more thoroughly about that. The club had focused on how-to volumes about finance. "Ana didn't seem to grasp the concepts," Lee told me. "She took detailed notes, but the questions she asked didn't address the issues we were all talking about."

"Did she attend for very long?"

"Three weeks, maybe. Frankly, I'm surprised she gave my name to you as a reference."

Janey Woodman? She'd known Ana the longest. Their high school years were long behind them, so why had Janey recently taken an interest in breaking Ana out of her shell? Janey hadn't struck me as a woman who needed old friends in her life; several people had greeted her enthusiastically in the coffee shop, and she'd introduced one of them to me as her "bestie." Of course, Janey also seemed to be the type who liked to be helpful.

Becca Sissel? She seemed sincere about wanting to help Ana, had indeed sent her the five thousand—unappreciated—dollars. But Ana had been upset with me for contacting Becca, claimed she would be "looking down her nose" at her. Why? Was there some dynamic there that I was missing?

* * *

Seven o'clock. I'd called Mark Evans earlier and when I'd mentioned Ana's name, he'd eagerly agreed to meet at Jude's Tavern. The club was on Van Ness Avenue, sandwiched between a new car dealership and a bank. Rock music filtered out onto the sidewalk, and the interior—as Ana described it—was hot, crowded, and noisy. Big-screen TVs showed reruns of football games in

10

three corners. I asked the hostess for Evans, and she pointed me to a booth near the rear.

Evans was sandy-haired, one of the baby-faced men who would never look old. He rose, asked what I would like to drink, and signaled to a waitress for my glass of wine. Then he asked eagerly, "Ana—is she all right?"

"She's had some difficulty." I explained about the cryptocurrency scam.

"Damn!" He slapped a hand on the table. "I should've warned her about investing in stuff like that! I'm an analyst for Citibank. I know the risks. But it never occurred to me that she would take that kind of plunge. Why did she?"

"Bad advice. Tell me, do you know anything about her friend Daniela?"

His mouth turned down. "The expatriate? Oh sure. Ana adores her. So free, she says. So worldly. But I can't imagine Daniela would set her up like that."

"Apparently, she didn't. But someone who could mimic Daniela convinced her to move her money."

"Someone who could mimic Daniela." He stared into the distance for a moment. "Let me check with a buddy of mine." He took out his phone, got up, and moved toward the door. "Be right back."

While I waited, I studied the crowd. They were a mixture of young and middle-aged, dressed in casual business attire. Long blonde hair predominated among the women; the men favored shorter cuts and were mostly clean-shaven. From the quality of their clothing—to say nothing of the prices on the drink menu—I assumed they were fairly affluent. They gathered in large booths or at long tables, calling out to friends and newcomers. At a nearby table, I spotted a pair of men, one at either end, holding an enthusiastic conversation with each other via their cell phones.

Mark was back in about five minutes. "Had to go outside; it's hard to make yourself heard in here. I was calling a friend of mine who's a sound engineer with one of the cable companies. He says it's easy to mimic a person's voice if you vary the levels and introduce enough background noise to distract the listener."

"Ana told me the connection was 'spotty'—one of the reasons she actually thought she was talking with Daniela in Paris."

"That could have been done deliberately."

"Did you ever meet Daniela?"

"No. Ana's always been very guarded about her friends."

"Someone also has told me that Ana never saved money."

"That I wouldn't know about. From her clothing, I'd say she spent a lot."

"She furnished my office with copies of statements from the various accounts that were looted."

Mark was looking bored with the conversation. "What I really want to know," he said, "is if there's a chance she'll come back to me. Money doesn't matter; I have plenty of my own."

"Why don't you ask her?" I surveyed the crowded bar, then blinked in surprise.

"How can I do that when she won't see me?"

"Look right over there." I gestured at a space near the hostess stand where Ana had suddenly appeared.

As I rose, Mark turned. When I reached the hostess, Ana had already slipped out the door.

* * *

She was nowhere on the street—not that I could have spotted her through the driving rain. I ran around the corner to where I'd parked my car, fumbled with my keys, and slipped inside, squeezing water out of my hair and reaching for a cap I kept in the back carrying space. I was severely pissed off at my client—so angry that normally I would have dumped her case on the spot. But not yet; it had piqued my curiosity, and I had too many questions to let them go unasked.

From the car I called Derek Ford. Still at the office, the unceasing workaholic. When I asked about the documents Ana had provided us, he said, "Can you come over here? There's something I want to show you."

Traffic from Van Ness to the financial district was slow on a rainy late afternoon. I drummed my fingers on the steering wheel and grumbled.

When I was finally seated across the desk in Derek's office, I pulled off my cap and used it to wipe moisture from my face. "So what have you found?" I asked.

He slid a sheaf of papers over to me. "Take a look at the numbers on these accounts," he told me.

They were the account statements showing zero balances that Ana had provided. I scanned them, shook my head. "They look okay to me."

"They're not. An extra zero has been added to each. No such account exists at any of the financial institutions. Someone's faked them to show no balances."

"Ana?"

"Most likely."

"But why?"

"Think, Shar, of what she's gained since she claimed to have been cleaned out."

I considered. "Glenn Solomon plans to pay her rent. Her interior decorator friend sent cash. Her flight attendant friend is offering frequent flyer miles in case she needs to travel to look for a new job. Her pal Janey gave her gifts from the store where she works and also offered her a place to stay. Her old boyfriend is determined to marry her."

"To say nothing of her getting free investigative services from M&R."

Dammit, I'd been had. Had like the most gullible victim of a simple scam.

I gritted my teeth, growled something along the lines of wanting to kill her.

Derek tried to hide a smile, but didn't quite succeed. "Don't get murderous," he said. "Get even."

We went to the conference room, met with my operatives Patrick Neilan and Julia Rafael, as well as my nephew Mick Savage, Hy, and a couple of operatives from his side of the business. Officer manager Ted Smalley obliged with a couple of pots of coffee. He also sat in and contributed avidly as we began to plan what we called Scamming the Scammer.

* * *

13

Ana called around noon the next day. "Sharon, I think I may have a line on the scammer."

"You *do?*" My surprised tone was disingenuous, given what I now knew.

"Yes. A man phoned this morning and claimed he knows who the woman is. He wants money before he'll tell me anymore."

"How much money?"

"He wouldn't say."

"Who is he?"

"He wouldn't tell me that either. He wanted to arrange a meeting."

"Where? When?"

"You know the Grove?"

It was a parklet near our building. An appropriate place, since the rain had yielded to a brilliantly clear day.

"Yes, I do."

"He'll be there at four-thirty. Can you come too?"

"Yes, but I may be a little late. Don't let that bother you, though; it's a perfectly safe location."

"I won't agree to anything till you get there."

You bet she wouldn't.

* * *

Our office manager, Ted Smalley, had volunteered to play the role of blackmailer and made the call to Ana last night. He'd really gotten into it, so much so that I'd had to ask him to tone down his villainous pose. A wiry, goateed man with streaks of silver in his dark hair, for years he'd indulged in periodic changes of costume: grunge, Edwardian, hip-hop, Botany 500, Hawaiian, caftans. You name it, he'd tried them all. Fortunately, under the influence of his husband, antiquarian book dealer Neal Osborne, he'd settled on more normal attire, although today, I'd had to restrain him from trading his coat for a cape worthy of Jack the Ripper.

I watched from the corner of our building as Ted crossed the parklet. Awnings had been let down over the little tables scattered there, and he approached the one where a slumped figure sat. Ana. From her posture, I assumed she wasn't taking the news of her "recovered money" well.

Ted's voice came over the open line between our cell phones. "Ms. Emery?"

"Yes."

"Ted Smalley. May I sit down?"

"If you wish."

Scraping of a chair as he sat.

"I understand you've been the victim of a cryptocurrency scheme."

"—One that you perpetrated."

"I'll neither confirm nor deny that."

"So what do you want?"

"To return your finds to you—for a percentage, of course."

"How much percentage?"

"Fifty."

She was silent.

I crossed the street, entered the parklet.

Ted went on, "I have here the most recent statements from your bank and brokerage accounts. Would you care to look at them?"

Grudgingly: "All right."

Rustle of papers.

"These aren't mine."

"It's your name on them."

"But they show the full balances that were scammed! They must be outdated."

"Look at the date—it's yesterday's." Yesterday's, when Derek had created them using actual statements as templates.

"But I gave my investigator the most recent statements."

"The most recently *doctored* statements."

"What does that mean? I don't know what you're talking about!"

More rustling of paper.

Ted said, "Look at the numbers on the statements you gave, er, your investigator."

Silence. Then: "Oh. There's an extra zero."

"Meaning the documents were faked."

"But who would do such a thing?"

I stepped up to the table. "Who, Ana? You."

She twisted in her chair, eyes wide with shock. "It's about time you got here. Who is this Ted Smalley person anyway?"

"A member of my staff. He volunteered to pose as a scammer."

"Why? And what's this about me faking those documents? Why would I?"

"To prove you'd been a victim of a scam."

"But *why?*"

"Because of the things you collected or are about to collect from people who care about you. Rent subsidies, cash, gifts, frequent flyer miles. And I've wasted a hell of a lot of my valuable time chasing around on your so-called case."

She pushed her chair back.

"Stay right where you are," I said. "There's no use rushing out and cashing in your accounts. I've already contacted the district attorney and he's put a hold on the funds."

She sank back, shaking her head. "I don't see why what I did was a crime. It was a game, that's all. Just a game."

"My agency has been playing a game, too. It's called Scamming the Scammer."

Twisted Sister

By Lori Armstrong

Oakwood University, Spring 1961

Two sharp knocks sounded on my dorm door, followed by "Thea. Phone!"

I pushed back from the desk and hurried out of the room, hustling down the hallway to the community phone cubicle. Picking up, I said, "On the line," waiting to hear the receiver click in the main reception room before speaking. "This is Thea Janis."

"Hello, Thea. It's Gigi Schaeffer. How are you?"

My heart raced. This could be it: Gigi was the VP of Kappa Gamma Xi sorority. Rush week had ended last week, and we were all anxious to find out if we'd been accepted into our first, second, or third sorority house choice. "I'm great. How are you?"

"I'm in a bit of a pickle, to be honest."

"Oh no. Is it something I can help you with?"

Gigi released a throaty laugh. "As a matter of fact, yes, you can. Are you busy right now?"

"Not really." The trigonometry homework on my desk called me a liar.

"Then, could you meet me on the third floor of the library?"

"Sure. When?"

"How soon can you get there?"

It'd take me at least ten minutes to cross campus. If I didn't have to doll up for the occasion and wear kitten heels. "I can be there in fifteen minutes, give or take."

"Perfect," Gigi purred. "This is a secret pledge mission. So tell no one where you're going. Oh, and dress for your work-study job."

My chest and neck heated. I hated that I'd had to disclose the cleaning duties that were part of my work-study scholarship on the rush application for the council. I had no idea how many sorority sisters knew about my financial circumstances. The candidate administrator had assured me that the applications were managed confidentially; only the sorority considering me as a PNM (potential new member) could access private information.

Did that mean Gigi had read my application because I'd been granted my first choice?

Or had she recognized me?

I returned to my room and opened the tiny door that hid my closet, stepping into the space in an attempt to keep my nosy roommate Betty Jean from initiating conversation. I hung up the emerald-hued cardigan and unbuttoned my cream-colored blouse.

"Who was on the phone?" Betty Jean asked.

Old me would've sniped "none of your business," but as I'd spent this year trying to reinvent myself, I merely clamped my lips together and didn't respond.

"Is this another stupid sorority thing?" Betty Jean said, the sneer in her tone grating. "God, Thea. Why do you even care to be part of their ridiculous little club? With their dress codes and old-fashioned rules?"

Pulling the gray smock over my head, I tugged the fabric past my hips. I didn't have time to change into the cotton skirt and rubber boots that completed my cleaning outfit; this wool A-line skirt and penny loafers would have to do.

"Not going to answer me?" Betty Jean prompted.

"Why do you keep harping about this?"

"Because we're friends." She swung herself around, dropping her sneakered feet to the floor. "You're being misled. Nothing is what it seems with that sorority."

"How do you know? I've never seen you with any of the sorority sisters. Never seen you at any of the Greek parties on campus."

"That is exactly my point, Thea. They take the 'secret society' mentality too far. They've done really horrible things to women who are—"

I held up my hand to stop her tirade. "No organization is perfect. I want to judge for myself, not listen to gossip and rumors."

Betty Jean snorted. "I know firsthand the rumors surrounding Gigi, the VP, and her puppet, Sheila, are lies to hide their nasty secrets."

A tiny kernel of curiosity sprouted. I'd never heard Betty Jean speak either of their names. She hadn't learned them from me since her toxic attitude toward sororities meant I avoided this conversation. But somehow, I'd gotten sucked into it again. "Look. I have to go."

"Fine. Just remember, we're here for an education and to become a better version of ourselves. Not to conform to their standards."

Sighing, I slipped on my black raincoat. "I have to conform, Betty Jean. I don't have connections to get decent internships or scholarship opportunities. Being a sorority member, I'll have more chances at bettering myself than I would without that designation. As an engineering major, you should understand that simple math." I flipped my hood up and strode out.

As I walked, my mind remained on the unusual situation my roommate and I were in—both twenty-year-old freshmen. Betty Jean, an army brat raised mostly overseas, had waited to attend college until her family returned to the States.

My enrollment situation was more complicated. I'd been born into a family with a bad reputation and even worse luck. My badge of honor? The lone family member who hadn't done jail time. Even when I'd tried to fit into the stealing/grifting family business, I hadn't been sent to juvenile detention— my shrewd mother had known if a cute little girl got caught pilfering cartons of cigarettes and bottles of cheap whiskey, the cops would return me home without the stolen goods and a stern lecture. Whereas if any of my brothers had been busted...a one-way ticket to boys' town awaited them, given our nefarious last name.

19

A last name I'd happily shed as soon as I'd turned eighteen.

It'd taken two years of working three jobs to save up enough money to attend college. That also allotted enough time to pass that I wasn't required to provide a transcript of my high school grades—no way to tie me to my former name and life. I studied for—and aced—the college entrance exam, paid the fees, and applied for additional financial assistance. Most days, I felt as if I'd pulled off the biggest con of any family member with this fresh start.

So maybe it was petty, shallow, and conformist that I sought entrance into a sorority. But it was something I wanted. Desperately.

In the library, I bypassed the main staircase and used the emergency exit stairs to reach the third floor, the least populated area for student hangouts since it housed the rare book collections and the librarian's administration offices.

Tucked away between the stacks, I caught a glimpse of Gigi's white-blonde hair.

I stopped behind her to catch my breath since I'd practically run the entire way.

She sensed me first and turned to face me. She wasn't beautiful, but she dressed and carried herself like a movie star—albeit a dime-store version of Marilyn Monroe. Shrewd eyes swept me from head to toe. Then she gestured to the seat opposite hers as if granting me an audience.

After I'd settled in, she leaned forward. "Thanks for coming, Dorothea."

I froze.

"Different hair color. New name." She smirked. "*Slightly* new name. Thea Janis, rather than Dorothea Janis Jenkins. Did you really think you'd be unrecognizable? Especially to me?"

Ice had formed on my vocal cords.

"I knew who you were right away." She paused. "You look just like him."

Him. Meaning my older brother, Donny. The guy she'd dated. Not that I'd ever hung out with her; our house wasn't the type of place Donny brought girlfriends.

"Please don't—"

Gigi held up her hand. "You can level just as much damage on me, as I can on you. I've spent six years becoming Gigi. I never want to go back to being Gladys Grace." She cocked her head. "After I learned you'd applied for rush, I scoured your application. No mention of Springdale anywhere."

"I haven't lived there for three years." I took a chance. "Is there mention of Springdale in any of your background?"

She shook her head. "I spent my first year at a junior college out of state. Then I transferred here, so everyone assumes I'm a local. You're the first person I've seen since I left there when I was sixteen."

"Same. No one in my family even knows where I am. And it's not like I have any plans to go back. Ever. Not after..." My mother and brothers had let Donny take the fall so our uncle wouldn't do the time and die in prison.

Her voice was whisper-soft when she asked, "How long is he in for?"

"Twenty-five years."

"I'm really sorry to hear that. Donny was great. I always thought..."

"He'd be the one to get out? Me too."

Gigi offered me a sympathetic look. "I'm glad you made your own way. Donny would be proud of you. And it's because of who you are that I asked for this favor."

"This favor has nothing to do with the results of rush week?"

"It does...in a way."

This isn't right. Make an excuse and leave.

But I didn't move. I waited.

"If you do this favor for me, as the VP of Kappa Gamma Xi, I can guarantee you an invite." She angled closer. "My friend Sheila, the membership chair, tallies the final votes."

"And...?"

"She will do whatever I tell her to do. If I say you're in, you're in."

Betty Jean's warning about Gigi and Sheila rang in my ears.

"Kappa Gamma is your first choice, isn't it?"

It was. Not even Gigi's presence and the fact she might've recognized me had kept me from listing it as my number one. Besides, Gigi was a senior. She'd graduate in a few weeks. Our college was one of the few that held rush week in the spring, rather than the fall. "I'll help you as long as whatever it is

21

you need me to do won't get me kicked out of school." I paused, narrowing my eyes. "You want me to steal something? Because that *is* what my family is known for."

"Actually, it's the opposite. I need you to leave a package someplace." She tucked her Monroe bob behind her ear and confided, "It's a super-secret prank I'm supposed to complete by myself, but I'm out of time."

"What's the prank?"

"Do you know Professor Amberson? In the English Department?"

"I know of him." Every female student knew of the dreamy professor with his dark good looks, enigmatic personality and ability to spontaneously spout a Shakespearean sonnet or a Lord Byron poem. His English Lit classes filled up immediately. Mostly with females.

"His 'in residence' office is in the building you clean."

"It is?"

"Yep. Corner office on the second floor."

"I never clean that room. Students aren't allowed in professor's offices."

"I know. I was his TA last semester. Cleaning his research office was part of my job. Anyway, the prank is to leave an envelope in a specific book and a note on his desk."

"You have a key to his office?"

"God, no. I wasn't allowed in that hallowed space unsupervised." The hardened, too-shrewd look in her eyes made me uneasy, and then she blinked it away. "I thought you'd have access to keys, being part of the cleaning crew."

I shook my head. "I'm only allowed to clean public spaces. The janitors are the key masters. Benny, the guy I work with, keeps his keyring clipped to his belt at all times."

"Oh." Gigi chewed on her lip. "That's a problem."

"Why? If you were Amberson's TA, can't you ask the janitor to let you in?"

"Amberson can't know I'm involved."

She squinted at me in a manner that made me feel…unwashed.

"What?"

"Didn't your Uncle Jimmy teach you how to jimmy locks?"

My face flamed. How much had my brother told her about our criminal upbringing? Because yes, I had learned that particular skill by the time I'd turned seven. I hated that she knew that about me. I hated even more that I *would* use that skill set for this favor if it got me one step closer to my goal of adding sorority sister to a resume.

"Look," she said with slight impatience, "the door handle is a simple lock. The deadbolt might be trickier, but thin wire used as a lockpick would work."

"If you know how to break in, why don't you do it?"

"Because, like I told you, it has to happen tonight when I'm at the Delta Phi party with Mick."

Mick was Gigi's boyfriend. I'd never met him personally, but everyone on campus knew who he was—a football-playing, hard-partying frat boy. Big money, big muscles, big focus on his social status. A guy nothing like my brother...then again, *Gladys* had dated Donny, not this polished, right-side-of-the-tracks Gigi. What had Donny called her? A pretty something.

"You still with me?" Gigi asked.

"Maybe." I studied her with the same coolness she'd given me. "Just trying to figure out if you're setting me up. If this is an initiation rite *I'm* supposed to pass." I mock-gasped, "I would never do something so morally wrong as breaking and entering, VP Schaeffer! Then, after you believe my outrage is real, you'll deem me worthy of the Kappa Gamma Xi invite."

Gigi rolled her eyes. "No. The VP from Theta Tau challenged me to this prank and I have to provide proof that I completed it. Which is why no one in kay gee zai knows about it."

Kay gee zai. Just shortening the sorority's Greek name sent a thrill through me. Like I'd already become a member of the club. "Fine. What am I putting in the office?"

From a sleek shoulder bag, she pulled out a manila envelope the size of a piece of typewriter paper. Sealed on both ends, with a string wound in a figure eight on the flap. She flipped it over, and an elaborately hand-lettered capital A in red ink filled the upper right corner. On top of that, she placed a smaller white envelope—also sealed, also with that artistic red A on the front.

She began to slide both across the desk but hesitated halfway. "Do I need to warn you not to open these?"

"No. I'm more concerned about how I'm going to get them inside the office than what's inside the envelopes."

Gigi smirked. "Just the Jenkins *what's in it for me* response I'd hoped for."

That arrogant little smile and the casual way she used my former surname with such condescension guaranteed I'd be looking inside both those envelopes. I'd suspected this situation had meant trouble for me, but she was the bigger fool if she thought I'd blindly follow her rules.

I half-listened to Gigi ramble about leaving the big envelope in the illustrated version of *The Scarlet Letter*, designated a special edition, located on the shelf behind the professor's desk, not to be confused with the regular edition, which was across the office on another shelf.

"Got that?" Gigi said, snapping me back to attention.

"Yes. I put the smaller envelope on the center of his desk where he's sure to notice it and took a pen as proof that I completed the task."

"My instincts were right. You're a natural at skulking around."

Did she believe I'd take that as a compliment? "Where am I supposed to bring the pen? To you at the party at Delta Phi tonight?"

Horror flashed in her eyes before she changed it into concern. "Oh no. We can't be seen together."

"Afraid I'll get caught, make a big scene, and rat you out?"

An even more uncomfortable look crossed her face. Or was that anger?

"I'm kidding. I won't get caught. Even if I did, I'm no snitch. That's a family trait, too." I winked. "But you do need proof, right? To give to Beta Nu?"

Gigi nodded. "The Beta Nu VP mentioned the professor's red pen as proof."

I honestly thought she'd be a better liar than this. Big difference between Theta Tau and Beta Nu, and not just that their names weren't similar enough to screw up. I'd made her repeat her error, just to be sure *I* wasn't mistaken. "You said time was a factor, and I'd hate for you to be ridiculed by another sorority for not completing your prank, so I'll bring the pen to the party." I held up my hand at her automatic protest. "Oh, it's no trouble at all since I'd planned to attend anyway. I'm sure no one would be suspicious of the *kay gee zai* VP merely speaking to a PNM at a social event," I said, smiling.

24

I stood and swept up both envelopes, tucking them in the inside zippered pocket of my rain jacket. "Anything else I should know about this favor?"

"Wait until after seven. Amberson will be gone."

On my way downstairs, I remembered what my brother Donny had called Gladys…the pretty pit viper. First to strike and slither away before you realize you've been poisoned.

* * *

I entered the Social Sciences Building at six forty-five. Benny didn't expect me tonight, so he'd be in the basement, listening to a baseball game. From the supply closet, I grabbed a flashlight and the big push broom in case I saw anyone, but the hallways were eerily quiet.

Amberson's office had no signage on the opaque glass window. I bent down and examined the door handle. I could pop that lock with the butter knife I'd liberated from the breakroom. The deadbolt would be harder, but it was in a good location, height-wise, for me to hear and feel when the pins clicked. My uncle had a set of bump keys that would've been perfect for this job, but I had to make do with bobby pins and paper clips.

Job. How easily the lingo returned.

This was a favor. Not a job.

Deep breath. Steady hands. Focus on the sound and vibration of metal.

I told myself not to look at the minute hand on my watch when I started.

I told myself not to look at the minute hand on my watch when I maneuvered the last pin into place.

But I did look.

Six minutes.

Not…terrible. But at age ten, it would've earned a round of bloody knuckles with my oldest brother, Bobby, for being too slow.

It took six seconds to pop the bottom lock.

Donny would've praised me for that and bought me ice cream.

Then I was inside the office, my heart racing with that adrenaline rush I hated.

God. I'd never wanted to feel this again. It was too damn addictive.

Pausing to calm down, I sat on the floor, gauging the space. Wide desk and chair in front of floor-to-ceiling bookshelves. Another bookshelf separated the back half of the room where a couch, chair and table were set up along the bank of windows covered by heavy draperies.

I pulled the envelopes from under my shirt. Pressed against my skin, my body heat softened the glue; no need to steam the seams to open the envelopes. More Jenkins' family tricks of the trade. I clicked on the flashlight and unwound the string on the manila envelope, then slipped the butter knife beneath the flap. It lifted up easy peasy.

Something was wedged between two sheets of thin cardboard. I gently pulled it out, and a stack of photos spilled all over the floor.

Cursing, I set the flashlight on its side as I gathered the pictures; the shocking images caused my cheeks to burn hot even in the cool darkness. So much for my seen-it-all attitude courtesy of my felonious upbringing. The images were of the professor and Gigi in sexual positions I hadn't even known were possible. Naked, half-clothed...on furniture, over furniture, *tied to furniture...*

Wait.

My gaze flew to the desk. Then, the chair. Then, the couch. All of the photos had been taken in this office.

Had the photo shoot been a mutual titillation thing?

Of course, it wasn't, Thea. Would Gigi have you secretly delivering these to him if they'd taken the photos together?

But someone *had* been in this room with them. Silently snapping pictures while they'd been performing naked sexual circus acts.

I studied the pictures from the photographer's viewpoint. Most were taken from the back wall. Several had been snapped from beneath the desk and shot up at—I slammed my eyes shut.

Nope. I did not need to see *that* image so closely again.

Leaving everything on the floor, I skirted the bookshelf and headed for the corner of the room. I hopped over the back of the couch, and...bingo. An adult could easily hide behind the curtain. From here, I realized a person could conceal themselves in the opposite shadowed corner or along the bookshelf that blocked one half of the room from the other half.

So, who would agree to take such pictures? They needed to be in place before the sexual shenanigans began. I doubted a person moving around the room would go unnoticed by the couple, no matter how deeply they were locked in the throes of passion.

The photographer either had to love Gigi or hate Amberson to agree to such a scheme.

Or maybe neither Gigi nor Amberson had known they were on kinky candid camera.

I returned to the pile I'd left on the floor and scooped up the pictures, replacing everything in the envelope. I breathed across the glue strip, pressing hard to reseal and winding the string around the clasp.

Flashlight in hand, I wandered behind the desk, scanning the shelves for an oversized edition of *The Scarlet Letter*. Amberson's organizational skills were atrocious for being an English professor—nothing was alphabetized. I found the book two shelves up. He'd never notice the envelope up that high, so I relocated the book to the shelf at chest level.

As tempting as it was to sit in the chair and read the folded note from the smaller envelope, I stood, holding the flashlight in one hand and the paper in the other.

I won't be used and discarded.

You know what I want.

Copies of these pictures will be given to the Dean of the English Department, the Faculty President, and the President of the College if you don't contact me by Sunday evening.

What do you think your chances of tenure will be then, Professor?

I replaced the note in the envelope, moistened my finger with spit, tracing the glue side of the envelope before pressing it down on the desk to reseal it.

I clicked off the flashlight and shoved it in my pocket.

Okay, so this wasn't a prank.

Gigi was blackmailing him.

But she'd been smart enough not to handwrite the note or deliver it here herself. Even if Amberson took it to the police, there wasn't proof *she'd* sent it, because would she really share such indecent photos of herself with all those college administrators?

Heavens, no. She'd been a victim. The photographer had invaded their privacy, but Amberson shouldn't have been in any of those positions with his TA in the first place.

The truth that she'd been a willing participant or even the instigator would get lost in the shuffle as he shouldered the blame for the sordid affair.

So what could Gigi want from him? Money? Or more money?

As I contemplated other options, I heard a sound that turned my blood cold: glass rattling in the door and keys in the lock.

I dove to the floor, scuttling like a cockroach, searching for the last patch of darkness. I'd just wiggled between the couch and the wall when the lights came on. I squinted above my head to see if the curtains were billowing, revealing my hiding place.

My heart hammered; blood whooshed in my ears, but I still heard the distinct sound of footsteps moving toward the desk. Then I realized there was a six-inch gap beneath the couch and I could see men's dress shoes.

I also saw a photo lying face-up that I'd missed picking up after the bundle had spilled on the floor. At least I hadn't left the knife, bobby pins, and flashlight beside it.

My family would be so disappointed in me right now. No ice cream for me.

The urge to giggle overwhelmed me, and I bit the inside of my cheek hard to stop it.

That's when the explosion of expletives echoed in the room.

Guess he'd found the pictures.

I'll admit disappointment that an English professor didn't have a more creative vocabulary when calling Gigi names. Then again, the crude ones for female anatomy did fit this scenario.

Amberson ranted and paced behind his desk for what seemed an eternity but was likely mere minutes. I heard him pick up the receiver on his phone twice, only to smash it back down both times.

We both startled when four loud raps vibrated the glass on his door.

"Professor Amberson?" a loud voice intoned with utterly false cheer.

A voice I knew all too well.

What on earth was *Betty Jean* doing here?

Click-click-click sounded across the stone floors as Amberson crossed to the door and opened it. "I'm sorry, I—"

"I didn't know you had an office in this building!" Betty Jean's familiar dirty white Chuck Taylor's moved into my line of sight.

"It's a separate space from my teaching duties, where I can write and research without interruption."

"I understand the need for privacy and quiet. My roommate gets on my nerves all the time."

Well, that wasn't nice. Wasn't true either. I was a lovely roommate.

"Wow. This is a great office."

"Thank you."

"Lots of space." She meandered to the side of the bookshelf. Stopped right in front of the dropped photo.

My stomach lurched. Was she *trying* to bring attention to it?

"Who are you?" Amberson demanded.

"Do you really think Shakespeare looked like the ponce in that painting?"

Amberson must've turned away to see what she'd pointed at, because she bent down and picked up the picture without missing a beat.

Oh, she was a sneaky one who'd just saved my bacon.

"Yes. I do. Again, I ask, who *are* you?"

"I'm Betty Jean Clarke. I was in your Intro to English Lit class last semester, remember?"

"Ah, right. Of course. Now I remember you."

"Anyway, my roommate cleans this building for her work-study, and I'm waiting for her. I wandered up here and saw you, so I thought I'd say hello." Pause. "So, ah…hello."

Awkward silence.

Awkward silences were very common with Betty Jean.

"You caught me when I'm in a bit of a rush, Betty Jean. I just popped in to

29

retrieve a book, and I'm actually late for a meeting."

"Oh. Sorry. I won't keep you. My friend should be done soon. She's hiding around here someplace."

Subtle was not Betty Jean's nature, but I got the message.

"I hope you find her."

"Me too. See you later, Professor."

"Good night."

Her shoes squeaked as she exited the room.

Amberson muttered and slammed things around. Then the lights went off, the door banged shut, and he engaged the deadbolt from the *outside*. So I knew he hadn't faked his departure to bust me when I emerged from my hidey hole.

Still, I remained in place and counted to three hundred.

Reversing course proved more difficult than diving in. I tore my skirt, scraped my knee, and ripped out a chunk of hair, courtesy of a wayward couch spring. As I attempted to put myself back together, I allowed for a quick detour to the desk. No surprise, both envelopes were gone.

Then I heard, "Psst, Nancy Drew. The coast is clear."

Didn't have to tell me twice.

As soon as I exited, Betty Jean grabbed me by the coat sleeve and dragged me out into the fresh air. Then she got in my face. "Are you trying to get kicked out of school?"

"No!"

"Then what were you doing?"

"I thought I was doing the VP a favor and guaranteeing an invite to Kappa Gamma. But I've just made things worse for me in ways you can't fathom." I feared Gigi would let my family know where I was. They'd come for me to drag me back and drag me down because no Jenkins ever turned their back on family…unless it suited them, of course, like it had with Donny.

"Look, don't get weirded out, but I followed you after you left the dorm. You and Gigi were whispering in the library, so the only thing I heard was seven o'clock. Since you already wore the cleaning smock, I figured you'd be coming here."

"Now who's Nancy Drew?" I grumbled.

"After you left, I followed Gigi. She met with Sheila on the second floor. They had a big fight, and Sheila left in tears. She refused to tell me anything."

My gaze narrowed. "You know Sheila?"

"Yeah."

"How?"

Betty Jean studied me. "We have the same proclivities."

Proclivities? "I thought she was a journalism major, not an engineer."

"God, Thea. It's not that hard to connect the dots." She exhaled. "Okay. Let's try it a different way. We're from the same island."

I frowned. "Island? Weren't you born in Germany? Unless you mean when your family was stationed in Japan?"

She placed her hands on my shoulders. "I was alluding to the Island of Lesbos. We're both lesbians."

"Oh. Oh!" I paused. I'd kind of suspected. "Are you and she…?"

"No. We're friends. We have our own club. It's too risky to pursue friendships with members outside of club time. So, normally, I wouldn't have approached Sheila, but I know the situation with Gigi, which is why I've been warning you to stay away."

"What can you tell me about it without breaking Sheila's confidence?"

Betty Jean blew out a breath. "Last year, before Gigi was named VP, she discovered that Sheila liked girls. She started blackmailing her. That's how Gigi got named VP; Sheila changed the vote totals after Gigi told that year's VP about another sister being a lesbian. The girl got kicked out of the sorority and had to change colleges. Gigi did all that just to prove to Sheila that she *would* rat her out if she didn't do whatever Gigi wanted."

My stomach twisted. "Does Gigi know about your club?"

"Not for lack of trying. Everyone in Kappa Gamma hates Gigi. She has a way of digging out people's secrets and then extorting things from them." She pulled out the picture she'd picked up in Amberson's office and playfully tucked it inside my coat. "Sheila has a camera and access to a darkroom, so I'll bet Gigi forced her to take these."

"That is horrifying. I mean, Amberson shouldn't have been diddling his

31

TA—"

"Wait, what did you say?"

"Gigi was his TA last semester."

Betty Jean laughed. "I was in Amberson's class. He refuses to have a TA. So Gigi got him drunk or something to get those photos. He's actually a decent guy. *She* is a monster. And you're not the only PNM doing her dirty work tonight. Five minutes after Sheila left, Gigi met up with two more hopefuls. One girl—that cute blonde with the freckles and weird name—is tasked with stealing Delta Phi's donation lockbox during the party. The other pledge is stuck typing both of Gigi's final term papers."

I paced away and walked back to Betty Jean. "How can we stop her?"

She shrugged. "Is killing her an option?"

"No, because we'd get caught."

Betty Jean threw her arm over my shoulder. "*You* would get caught since you left a trail straight into Amberson's office tonight."

"I did not!"

"You propped a broom against the wall next to the door. I stepped on two broken paper clips that you used to open the lock. And you forgot to pick up a picture from the floor. You're lucky Amberson didn't see that or the tips of your shoes poking out from behind the couch. You'd make a terrible criminal, Thea."

I knocked her arm away but sent her a genuine smile. "That's the nicest thing anyone has ever said to me."

* * *

We walked back to the dorm, shared a quick snack, a couple of laughs, and parted ways.

After hearing what Gigi had done to others, I knew her plans for me. I had to stop her before she contacted my family. I gathered what I needed and returned to the Social Sciences Building.

Benny snored in the breakroom and didn't move when I lifted his bottle of brandy.

I zipped up my raincoat and tightened the hood, donned a pair of plastic gloves, wrapped a new, heavy-duty cleaning cloth over my mouth and nose before slipping into the supply room. Benny didn't take these precautions when baiting traps, but I'd opted to use an old family recipe with triple potency, passed down from my mother. After I finished mixing it, I stripped, wiped myself down, washed the outside of the flask, and changed into clean clothes.

Then, I showed up at the Delta Phi party.

Everyone was in a celebratory mood. I mingled, exchanging hugs with a few girls who were PNM hopefuls for Kappa Gamma and other sororities. Talked about finals with guys from my trig class. Normally, I would've flirted with a frat brother or two, but I kept moving, staying out of Gigi's view while keeping her in mine.

The only time I lost sight of her was when I saw Monique, the blonde that Betty Jean had mentioned, dart up the stairs. I followed her.

Poor girl had no idea what she was doing or where she was going. Bouncing down the hallway like an out-of-control pinball had already garnered her odd looks from the partygoers. I said, "Monique? Are you okay?"

She spun around. "Thea. Sorry. I have—"

I shoved her into an alcove. "No matter what Gigi is holding over your head, doing this prank won't guarantee an invite to Kappa Gamma, but it could get you kicked out of school. Think about that before doing something you can't undo."

"I'm scared. I don't want to be part of a sorority that expects me to steal."

"*Gigi* expects it, not Kappa Gamma. All the secrets and lies she's perpetuating will be over after she graduates."

"What should I do?"

"Avoid Gigi and go back to the dorm. Continue like none of this happened." She nodded and hugged me before she took off.

When I exited the alcove, I spied Sheila down the hall, lounging against a door, smoking a cigarette, eyeing me through a crowd of revelers.

I approached her warily.

A plume of smoke curled from her vibrant red lips. "Gigi finds out you warned Monique off, there'll be hell to pay." She inhaled and exhaled. "Then again, Gigi pocketed the money from the strongbox an hour ago, so she doesn't need a fall girl anymore."

I rested against the wall next to her. "She's the devil, isn't she?"

"You don't know the half of it. But I'll fill you in because I graduate in two weeks, and someone needs to know the truth." Another deep drag. "Our Gigi is a real piece of work. Earned her first major payoff at age sixteen when she threatened to tell the police that the minister at their family church raped her, got her pregnant, and she lost the baby. But that forced the family to move. Then she pulled the identical scam with her new boyfriend, but after he paid the hush money, Gigi's own family washed their hands of her. That's how she ended up by her little lonesome at this college.

"Gigi's extortion schemes are who she is, whether it's extracting information, money, goods or services. She's never paid her own tuition or sorority fees, someone else always covers it as a 'favor' to her. She skates by with a C average, which is a surprise since she doesn't do her own homework. If someone doesn't buy or give her clothes, she steals them. Either from a sister, from a store, or has a sister steal them from another sister or a store. She has information on anyone she deems important, and she'll use it—and them—to her own ends. This semester she's got five administrators providing her kickbacks in some form. I know that because she forced me to help her set up three of them."

"How does she get away with it?"

Another inhale and exhale. "Easier to go along to get along, I guess. Some people, like me, actually have higher life stakes for ruination if we don't do her bidding." She gave me a sidelong glance. "She plans to send a letter to your family in whatever backwoods area y'all are from. Letting them know you changed your name and where to find you."

Anger churned, and I fought to remain calm. "Has she sent the letter yet?"

"Nah. She's a mean cat who wants to toy with her new mouse some more." Sheila ground out her cigarette in the ashtray beside the door.

"Is there any way to stop her?"

"Besides murder? None that I can see."

"Betty Jean said the same thing."

Sheila smiled savagely. "A lot of us think that. Some of us even say it, but no one does anything."

"Maybe that'll change."

A commotion started downstairs.

"That's my cue." Sheila took two steps, then faced me. "For what it's worth…Kappa already voted you in. It's been posted, so she can't change the results. But don't think she can't inflict major damage on you before she leaves."

I let that comment firm my resolve before I headed toward the sound of breaking glass and men yelling.

From my vantage point on the stairs, I saw two guys fighting. Both bloodied, one looming over the other. A crowd had gathered, but no one intervened.

When the bigger guy backed up a step, I saw it was Mick, Gigi's boyfriend. "I can't believe you touched her. You're supposed to be my best friend!"

The other guy, obviously drunk, held up his hands and tried to reason with Mick. "I *am* your best friend. I never touched her. She's lying."

"Yeah? And did she rip her own dress, too?" he pointed at Gigi, cowering behind him.

Gigi's bodice hung open, buttons missing, the lace of her pink bra visible. "I didn't do that! I swear!"

I realized the drunk one was Hank Fox, the President of Delta Phi.

"Mick. Listen. I don't understand—"

"I do. You've always wanted what I have. Including her." Letting loose another roar, he punched Hank in the stomach, knocking him to his knees. "But I'm done with you. And you can say goodbye to the internship with my dad's firm this summer, too."

"No. You know I need that internship. It's the only way I can…please." Hank, still on his knees, tried to grab Mick's legs, but Mick knocked him down.

"Don't do this to me. Please." Hank started crying. "I'm sorry. I…"

Everyone's focus was on Hank.

Mine stayed on Gigi. The triumph in her eyes made me ill.

After delivering a final "You disgust me" to Hank, Mick turned to Gigi and kissed her forehead.

She nodded at whatever he'd whispered in her ear. She leaned on Sheila, as if needing support.

Then Mick returned to his buddies.

The party didn't break up, but Hank's friends had taken him away.

I didn't hide from Gigi. I let her see me having a raucous time. Laughing. Flirting. Dancing. Being the carefree college girl, I never dreamed I could be. Something she wanted to take away from me just because she could.

I sensed her agitation that I was there.

Occasionally, I tipped my flask, always when she watched me, never offering a sip to anyone else.

When I stepped outside to cool off, she followed me into the dark corner I'd chosen.

Pretending to be too tipsy to notice was too easy.

"Hey, Jenkins."

I whirled around sloppily, wild-eyed. "Ssh! It's Janis, remember?"

"My mistake." She sauntered forward. "Why are you still here?"

"Just having fun. Been a crazy stressful night, you know?" I winked with drunken exaggeration.

"How much have you been drinking?"

I hid the flask behind my back. "A little bit."

"Come on now, Dorothea. I've been watching you. You've had enough. Hand over the flask."

"No! It's umm...empty anyway."

Gigi laughed meanly. "Then it shouldn't be a big deal to give it to me."

With reluctance, I handed it to her, hoping my instincts were right.

She shook the flask. "Doesn't sound empty."

"Fine. I know you're just gonna waste it and dump it out."

"Now, why would I do that? I noticed you weren't sharing with your friends, so it's higher quality stuff than the swill they're drinking, isn't it?"

I refused to answer. Held my breath and glared at her as she twisted off the cap, lifted the flask, and drained every drop.

She licked her lips and handed it back. "Not bad. A little bitter for my taste."

"That's what my dad said, too."

Right before he died.

"It's late, you'd better get going."

"Sure. Gotta use the ladies first." I swayed and turned around. "Wait. Wasn't I supposed to give you that proof thing?"

Gigi feigned confusion. "What?"

"The proof. From the favor I did for you tonight."

The hair flip, pursed lips, narrowed eyes response was an over-the-top reaction even for her. "I have no idea what you're babbling about. Lay off the booze, Dorothea. It's always been your family's downfall." She slithered away.

I ditched the flask deep in the overflowing trash can and returned inside to complete my last task.

Moody Mick lumbered up the stairs, drunkenly swaying with each step.

I pretended to lose my balance and fell against him, hugging him close so I could slip the folded picture into his pocket. "Oh, I'm so sorry. My foot slipped."

He snarled, "Move it," and shook me off.

I wished I could be a fly on the wall or a mouse in the corner as the rest of the night's events unfolded, but the spikes of adrenaline had taken a toll, and exhaustion set in.

I scarcely remember the walk back to the dorm. I forced myself to take a very hot shower and crawled into bed, falling into a dreamless sleep.

* * *

I spent all day the following day in the Social Sciences Building. Cleaning, shooting the breeze with Benny, studying for finals, but also biding my time, hoping my cocktail had taken effect. I didn't return to the dorm until almost nine o'clock that night.

Betty Jean pounced on me the minute I entered the room. "God, Thea.

Where have you been?"

"Working and studying. Why?"

"Did you hear that Gigi Schaeffer was found dead?"

"No!" I gasped in shock and sat down hard on my bed. "Do they know what happened?"

She plopped down beside me. "Her body was discovered about two o'clock this morning, halfway between the Delta Phi and Kappa Gamma houses. It's been crazy. Anyone that knew her or saw her yesterday had to go to the police station and answer questions."

"Why?"

"Because she was murdered."

My jaw dropped. "Murdered? How?"

Betty Jean studied me. "That's the strange thing. The cops don't know."

"What do you mean they don't know?"

"She had multiple injuries."

"What do you mean multiple injuries?" I sounded like a parrot.

"This is what I heard from Sheila, who was with the group that found her. Apparently, Gigi had been strangled." She paused. "And stabbed and bludgeoned and kicked. She was missing an eye, which might've been removed by force or could've been pecked out by birds—not sure on that one. But whichever way had killed her, more than one person added to her bodily injuries to make sure she was really dead...*after* she was clearly already dead."

Stupefied, I just blinked at her because that wasn't what I'd expected to hear *at all.* I couldn't ask if Gigi's skin had also been discolored or if she'd also been found in a pool of her own bloody vomit or if her insides had also turned into goo. I wasn't one hundred percent certain what arsenic did to a person, besides kill them.

But I hadn't killed her. Someone else had beat me to it. Quite literally.

God. I really was a lousy criminal.

"Thea?"

I refocused. "Sorry. What?"

"It is shocking, isn't it? I mean, the gruesomeness of it, but not the fact it happened to her. Gigi had doubled down in recent weeks, trying to squeeze every last penny out of her marks before she graduated, and someone had had enough. I wonder who finally mustered the guts to do it."

"Do the police have any suspects?"

Betty Jean snorted. "Everyone at Kappa Gamma. Everyone at the other sororities. Half of her current and former instructors. Mick. Hank Fox. Amberson. People at the party." Another pause. "Wait. *You* were at the party."

"For about twenty minutes until I saw Monique and told her to go back to the dorm. I did see Mick humiliate Hank over something he'd supposedly done to Gigi, but that scene was too much for me, and I left."

"Guess you missed the big blow-up between Mick and Gigi. He found one of those blackmail pictures of Gigi and Amberson and lost his temper. Threatened to kill her. She ran out of the Sigma Phi house around midnight and that's the last time anyone saw her alive."

"Huh. No wonder he's a suspect."

"So I have to ask, Thea, what happened to the picture I found last night in Amberson's office that I gave back to you?"

I met her stare. "I have no idea. I must've lost it someplace."

Betty Jean gave me a considering look and stood. "Oh, another weird thing Sheila told me. When the police called Gigi's next-of-kin? The phone had been disconnected. The family moved and didn't leave a forwarding address. Looks like Kappa Gamma Xi will get stuck burying Gigi once the cops release her body."

"I wonder how long before that'll happen?"

"I bet they want to get rid of her pretty quick. She's got no family; the college looks stupid for all the financial schemes she had going, and the cops have at least twenty suspects with motives for wanting her dead. Not one person has stepped forward in her defense. Not one. What does that tell you?"

That the cops won't waste resources doing postmortem bloodwork so no one will find out that I poisoned her a few hours before she was strangled, stabbed, bludgeoned, and kicked to death.

"Thea?"

I shrugged. "That a lot of people will sleep easier tonight."

She groaned. "I'm being serious."

"So am I."

Two weeks later...

A sharp knock sounded on my dorm door, followed by, "Thea. Phone!"

I pushed the packing box next to the desk and hustled to the community phone cubicle. I picked up and said, "On the line," waiting to hear the receiver click in the main reception room before speaking. "This is Thea Janis."

"Hey, little sis."

My heart leapt. "Donny? Is it really you?"

"Yep."

"I can't believe you're calling me! How are you?"

"I'm all right. Miss you."

"I miss you too. Every day."

"Good to know, but I'm glad you don't come around and see me like this." Tears welled up. "It's not your fault."

"That's the only thing that keeps me goin' some days. Anyway, I ain't got long to talk. You and me have always been square with one another, yeah?"

"Yeah."

"You oughta know...Gladys called me."

"When?"

"Bout a month ago. Pretended to be you to get me on the line."

"Miserable lying witch," I muttered.

He laughed. "Got that right. She cut right to the chase. Said she planned on telling the family they oughta be proud of you, college girl living it up in the big city. Said they probably missed you all the years you'd been gone so she'd let them know where you were right away so they could visit."

"What'd you say?"

"Nothin'. But actions speak louder than words, so I handled it."

A tingle started at the base of my neck. "But she's..."

"The way she oughta be. Outta the picture. She's never gonna write that letter or make that call, so you're in the clear."

"But...how? You're in there."

"Don't mean that I don't got friends out there who owe me a favor. And rumor was, she was *neck deep* in trouble anyway."

I laughed at his morbid pun. Now I knew who'd strangled her, even if by proxy. It'd been a grave mistake on Gigi's part to taunt a man in prison. He had nothing to lose, and he'd do anything for the sister, who had everything to gain.

"Thank you."

"Thank me by makin' something of yourself. That's the other thing that keeps me goin'; knowing you got out."

"I will. It's come to my attention that I'm really bad at the family business."

"Happy to hear that, little sis."

"I knew you would be."

$400 Gets You Elvis

By Libby Cudmore

L ars ran a handful of pomade through their hair. They hoped no one would notice just how shitty this dye job was. That's what they got for doing it in the sink in their apartment. Some things are best left to a professional. But when you're paying $25 to see an Elvis impersonator on a Thursday morning in a fake Las Vegas studio set up in what used to be a Ruby Tuesdays, you can't complain about a bad dye job. Their cut of those $25 tickets didn't pay for much more than boxed dye.

Rich knocked on their door. "I need a big favor," he said. "Dolly called in sick, and we need a witness for a wedding. Can you fill in?"

"What time?"

"Two o'clock," he said. "You can make it if you cut a few songs from your Elvis brunch. Laura said you can use her costume. You don't need to sing, just need a witness on the bride's side. Groom's brother is going to stand in by him."

"Can't Caroline do it?"

"Caroline has Easter Bunny hours," he said. "At least until Joe sobers up."

"I'd rather be the Easter Bunny."

"I'll give you an extra $75. Most witnesses only get $50."

"Elvis gets $400."

"When he officiates," Rich said. "Do you want to be Dolly or not?"

$75 could get this dye job fixed. It was just another costume, they told

42

themselves. Just another act. They could perform in fake tits and a gown for a few minutes. Hell, they'd performed femininity for most of their life, but no one paid them $75 to get dressed up for Christmas parties and prom night. They just had to make sure they got all that makeup off. The King didn't wear glitter eyeshadow.

* * *

The bride, Pauline, was waiting in the wedding suite. She had her hair in a claw clip and a face full of Wet & Wild make-up, the free white *Bride* shirt that came with package #2. She smiled when she saw Dolly, but she was clutching her silk flowers nervously. Dozens of other brides had clutched those same silk flowers, a something-borrowed from the Little Vegas wedding closet. She had on a veil tiara from the party store down the block. Not even the rhinestone one, a plastic bachelorette party crown with a whisper of tulle hanging off the back.

"I've always wanted to go to Las Vegas," Pauline said, glancing around the room at all the pixelated posters of the Bellagio and the Strip. "The real one, I mean. Not even to gamble. Just to see the lights. Or maybe I could play a slot machine, just once, and come up a winner with all those quarters pouring out like a waterfall. Just once."

Lars had been to NYC. To Atlantic City. But never to Vegas. Vegas was a step too far. Everyone went to Vegas to win, and almost all of them lost. They'd never pass for a Vegas Elvis at even the cheapest buffet. At least this was steady work, paid the rent, left a little for costume upgrades. Besides, Elvis acts were a dying breed, remembered more for kitsch than for music. They could add a few more characters to his roster; lip synch to Maroon 5 for suburban moms, become Prince Charming or Batman for birthday parties, Bowser or Godzilla in a hot foam suit. There were other possibilities. They just didn't like any of them.

"You must see a lot of brides," she said. "Are they always this nervous?"

They patted her hand. "Every single one," they drawled in Dolly's honey-thick accent. "A wedding is a performance, and you want to do it right. It's just stage fright, honey."

"Thank you," she said, squeezing tight. "You know, I always pictured my wedding at a church, with a pastor and all my friends, but I guess if I had all that, then I couldn't tell my co-workers that I had Dolly Parton as my bridesmaid."

"You know, honey," they said. "You don't have to do this right now. If you want a church wedding, I'll still come be your bridesmaid. Or we'll get you an Elvis. I know the King personally. I bet I could even get you a discount."

"No, this is just fine," she said. "Brett isn't into all that kind of fancy shit, and besides, those weddings cost a lot of money. We were dropping off some cans at the refund place, and we found this place. He dropped to one knee, and he asked me right there in the middle of the Can Man! It's perfect. Romantic, you know?" She wiggled her ring finger, a Walmart gem catching the lamplight of the dim little room.

"How long have you two been dating?"

"Seven months," she said. "And I was thinking about leaving him—we've been fighting a lot lately, but then he proposed, and I thought, well, why not? He said if we do this today, we can save up and have a big party with our friends next year. I'll be sure to invite you."

There wouldn't be a big party. They'd seen brides come through here two years later with a new guy and the same dress. They'd seen grooms request the cheapest package so they could get hitched before shipping off to bases and ports unknown. But they couldn't tell Pauline that. "I'd love that," they said.

Pauline forced a smile that cut through her tears. "Stage fright," she repeated.

It would be easy to tell her to just walk out the door and never come back, leave her impulsive groom, and vanish. Where would she go? She clearly didn't have family if she was asking Dolly Parton to be her bridesmaid, no friends to take her in, either. Hell, she might be pregnant already. But Dolly wasn't paid to give advice. Dolly was paid to sing and smile and stand still when asked. And besides, if the wedding was called off, The Little Vegas Chapel gave a full refund. They needed that money. Their rent was coming due soon.

Pauline dabbed her eyes with a whisper-thin tissue. She squeezed Lars' hand once more.

"C'mon honey," they said. "Let me put some curls in your hair."

* * *

The CD of wedding music started. Pauline took a deep breath and missed her first step. Brett wore his *Groom* shirt with faded black jeans. His brother was at his side; he smelled like weed and twitched like coke. He stared at Dolly's fake tits with a mixture of disgust and desire. He kissed his bride with too much tongue, even as she squealed and squirmed and tried to get away.

The Little Vegas Wedding Chapel didn't specialize in happy marriages. Photo shoot with the background of the strip cost extra. Use our flowers or bring your own. $400 gets you Elvis.

* * *

Two months went by before they saw Pauline again. She crept into the back of one of their Frank Sinatra shows. Her drugstore makeup couldn't hide her black eye. She clapped but they could tell she'd been crying. They looked lovingly at her while they crooned "Fly Me To The Moon," knelt at her feet and handed her a fabric rose. She beamed through concealer and tears, but left before the photo opp.

The next time she showed up, they were doing Elvis, hips swaggering, voice deep and throaty. This is where they felt real. Not as Dean or Frank or Bobby Darin, certainly not as Billy Joel with the tunes programmed into the keyboard. When they were 10, their grandma took them to see an Elvis impersonator in Atlantic City; she screamed in a way that they had never heard their grandma scream. Like that man was the real Elvis. And Lars was caught up in the spectacle, the space that existed between his sneer and his sequins. This was their destiny. This is who they wanted to be. They combed their hair into a pompadour, cuffed their jeans, practiced the snarl and hip shake in the mirror. Their grandmother hired them to perform for her gardening club banquet, paid $50 for them to lip-synch and say *A-thankya, a-thankya much* to the ladies. Her memory, they thought, was the only thing that got them on stage every night. That and the rent.

Pauline stayed until everyone else had left. She drank a banana daiquiri at the bar, and when they got changed, she asked if she could buy them a drink.

"I don't know if you remember me," she said. "You were my bridesmaid a few months ago. You were Dolly then."

"I remember."

She took a sip of her daiquiri. The bartender brought Lars a post-shift drink, a vodka tonic that was far too heavy on the tonic. Watered-down drinks for a watered-down show. At least their dye job was better this time. That $75 had come in handy.

Paulina waited until the bartender was elsewhere. She took a longer drink and lowered her voice. "I've just killed my husband," she said. "And I need your help."

* * *

Lars cooked up a few of the leftover sirloins in the back of the kitchen after everyone else had gone. Paulina sat on the kitchen counter, eating after-dinner mints by the handful, straight from the six-pound bag. "I want to say things got worse," she said. "But the truth is they were bad from the start. I don't even know what worse might look like. Until tonight."

It wasn't enough to knock her around a few times, she told them. To come home drunk, if he came home at all. But this time, he brought his brother, the same one who stood by his side on his wedding day. She didn't go into details. She didn't have to.

"Why tell me?" they asked.

"Because you're the only friend I've got."

No one would have blamed Lars if they said no. They didn't owe this woman anything. Hell, another three months and they might not have even recognized her, let her fade from memory like all the other brides and grooms

46

that had come and gone through the fake-flower arch of the Little Vegas Wedding Chapel. The cops could handle this.

But they wouldn't.

Four years ago, one of the grooms had beaten his second bride into a coma. The papers said she'd tried to have him arrested a few times, but they always released him, called it a domestic, and let him go home. But she never went home. Last anyone knew, she was living in a group home with no idea who she once was, unable to walk, unable to feed herself. The groom pled guilty, got twenty-five years. But the bride had a sentence so much longer than that. Hers was a life sentence, her own body, her prison.

They sighed. "I've got an idea," they said. "C'mon, let me do your hair."

* * *

It was hard to tell what color Pauline's house once was. Yellow, perhaps, or a warm gray. Now it was weather damaged, paint and wood peeling, missing shingles like rotted teeth.

Pauline sat in the passenger seat. She scratched around her fake beard. "How do you do this?" she asked. "It itches so badly."

"I don't," they said. "It was from an abandoned Sonny and Cher act. Our Cher got a better offer doing dinner theater in Poughkeepsie."

"I don't see why I have to get dressed up," she said. "There aren't any cameras and no neighbors for another mile in either direction."

"Traffic cams," they said as they got out of the truck. "Neighbors who might have seen the car. They need to believe two men were driving. They can't know you were ever here. They need to believe you left and didn't come back."

She followed Lars out and inside. Brett was slumped in the chair, a worm of blood dried beneath his nose. Another man was passed out face-down on a curbside couch, vomit dried into the plaid weave. The brother. They were both dead. "What did you do?" they asked.

"Rat poison," she said with an ease, as though they'd asked the secret ingredient in her chocolate chip cookie recipe. "In their cocaine."

There were baggies and scales in the kitchen. They hated the thought that there was money somewhere, money they could use. Brett wouldn't miss it. "Where's the cash?" they asked.

"There isn't any," she said. "Brett always thought of himself as some big-time gangster, but the truth was that he was snorting more than he sold."

They caught a glint of the ring on her hand. It was bigger than the one she got married with, a real diamond and gold that had a jeweler's sheen. "My mother's," she said. "I never take it off. He threatened to chop off my hand and sell it. That's when I knew I was in real danger. That's when I knew I had to...."

They understood. They used to love dressing up in their grandmother's diamond bracelets and emerald rings and pearl earrings. She always said there had been more, so much more, but she had to sell it to get away from her first husband. Later, their father had to sell it to pay for her nursing home. Lars stole a pair of her ruby earrings and had them made into cufflinks. They were glad they had them in their costume case. There wouldn't be time to go back to their apartment.

"Get a garbage can," they said. "And fill it with paper. Toilet tissue, newspapers, anything that can burn."

She obeyed. While she was gone, they peeked in the freezer, the coffee can, anyplace that might have a stack of twenties they could make their getaway with. Nothing to take with them, not even a bag of pretzels for the road.

Pauline returned with the bathroom trash and a half-emptied bottle of cheap tequila. There was a pregnancy test in there. Positive. She saw them looking. "Don't worry," she said. "It was a virgin daiquiri. I don't want liquor to ever pass my baby's lips. I just thought this might come in handy."

Pauline had read their mind. "Go outside and get into the truck," they said. "I don't want the smoke to hurt the baby."

Lars lit a cigarette with the lime green Bic. They savored the scent for a minute, never mind that there were dead bodies at his feet, never mind that the room smelled like liquor and vomit and shit. That smell would always remind them of their grandmother. They never told their father what she said when he was out of the room, a morphine haze rendering her capable of telling the truth in a way life never let her. *Lila*, she said. *I don't regret killing my husband. I just wish I'd done it sooner.*

They weren't mad. They weren't scared. They didn't even care that she used their deadname. They loved her more in that moment than ever before. They loved her for what she had endured, what she had risen up from, with an infant on her hip, a bottle of sleeping pills, and a box of matches. This moment, more than Elvis, was how they could honor everything she had taught them.

They took a swig from the tequila bottle. *To you, Grandma Bernadette*, they said. They emptied the bottle into the trashcan and dropped in the cigarette. It sparked and smoldered and lit, melting the plastic sides. For a moment, they were mesmerized by the flames. For a moment, they wanted to watch it all burn.

"Now what?" Pauline said when they got back in the truck.

"Now," they said. "We head to Vegas."

* * *

They dumped Paulina's beard and the clothes they were wearing in a gas station garbage bin. They loaded up on sandwiches and snacks and bottles of water. They could make it in three days if they took turns driving and only stopped to gas up, avoided toll roads and traffic cameras as much as they could.

She finally spoke on the edge of Ohio. "I bet you think I'm an idiot for marrying him," she said.

"I don't think you're an idiot," they said. "I just wondered what you saw in him. He was so shitty to you on your wedding day."

"Have you ever been in love?"

"Never once." They never felt that tug, that urge, that need to lose themselves in another person. *One day you'll meet someone*, their mother always said, as thought it was a problem that could be fixed with speed dating or an app. Lars went on dates. They went to bars, had drinks, hooked up. But it was never love. It was barely desire. After awhile, they got comfortable

49

with not even trying.

"You're not missing anything," she said.

"Did you love him?"

"More than anything," she said. "I was crazy about him, but he was just crazy. I thought, *maybe if I just love him enough*, he'd transform, like the end of *Beauty and the Beast*. But I'm not Belle, and my best friend isn't a damn clock. My best friend wouldn't even come to my wedding. Said I was making a mistake, and she couldn't watch." She glanced over at them and smiled. "But my best friend wouldn't have helped me escape either. So I guess it worked out."

"I guess so."

Another 100 miles stretched before she spoke again.

"Are you going to still be Elvis when you get to Vegas?" she asked.

"I hope so," they said. "What about you?"

"I'm not sure," she replied. "Maybe I'll pull that slot machine, win a million dollars, and not have to do anything for a while. Have my baby and buy her nice things."

"You know it's a girl?"

"Of course, it's a girl," she said. "And I'm going to name her Suzanne, and she is going to have the best life. Better than the one I left behind. She's not going to marry some drug dealer because he promises her he has money to take care of her. She'll be able to take care of herself."

"Is that what he told you?" they asked. "Just a few more sales, and we'll get out of here?"

"Like a shitty movie," she said. "Love is blind, sure, but love is also dumb as hell sometimes. I guess I just wanted to feel special to someone."

They knew that feeling. *Just another six months*, they'd told themselves twice a year. *Another few shows, and then I'm gone*. But night after night, show after show, they packed up and went home to that same studio apartment. Now they were two lost souls—three if you counted Suzanne—on the open road, headed to Vegas to get even more lost. Hard lives behind them. They didn't want to think about what she'd endured in that house or how she got pregnant. But they couldn't help but be worried about what she'd have to endure in Vegas. What if she got suckered in by another sweet-talking scumbag?

"Pull over and let me drive for a while," she said. "How about you get some rest?"

* * *

They were outside of Oklahoma City when they dared to check the news back home. The fire department had responded to the fire at Brett's far too late; two bodies burned beyond recognition, no one to claim them. No one to put out a missing persons report on Pauline. Some people can just up and leave. Just like their grandma had after the fire. Sell some jewelry, pack up some bags, start over somewhere else. They hoped their grandma would be proud that they helped out a damsel in distress.

Lars called the Little Vegas Wedding Chapel from a burner phone and left a message. Said they were sorry. Said they got an opportunity elsewhere. Said they'd send for their check when they landed and left no number to call back on.

Back in the car, and they drove through the night.

* * *

They arrived around noon and got a $21 hotel room at Circus Circus. They slept twelve hours with their backs to each other in the queen-sized, gorged on the buffet downstairs, and went back to sleep. Lars thought they heard her showering sometime in the night. Or maybe it was just a dream. Maybe all of this was a dream and they would wake up back in their little studio apartment in Rotterdam, New York, a long night of pomade and eyebrow pencil sticky on their pillow. But when they woke up, they were still in Vegas. They were still with Pauline. And they were still on the lam, just as they would be for the rest of their lives.

They sold the truck to a dealer outside of the city, a man who said he'd take care of the plates and the title. He told them he knew a guy who could get them new lives, too. Fake IDs and bogus social security numbers. They were now officially Lars Konstanty, their grandmother's maiden name. Pauline was now Paula Hart. "Easier to remember," she said, giggling. "Wouldn't want to give myself up."

They took a cab to the Strip. Even in the daytime, it was more than they could have imagined, more than the glamour shots and outdated posters hung on the walls of the Little Vegas Wedding Chapel. The Bellagio fountains. The Mirage and The MGM Grand and the High Roller. Everything their grandma wanted to see in her life. And there they were, right in the center of all of it.

"It's beautiful, isn't it?" she asked. "It's like Heaven."

For a moment, they thought about asking her to stay. They could get a little place, raise the baby together. But they knew that would never work. They had to go their separate ways. They had to start over, and that meant starting over apart. They had been strangers, briefly friends, and now strangers again. Just like the audiences they played, night after night—familiar faces sharing a moment, but like the water spurting from the fountain, it was just for a moment before it all went away.

Paulina—Paula—reached into her bag and pulled out a roll of hundreds as big around as a coffee cup. "Here," she said, peeling off half. "Thanks for the ride."

So that's where all the money in the house went. She'd kept it from them for safety, for power. She might have even killed Brett and his brother for it. And she held onto it while their savings dwindled down on gas and snacks and the bottomless cups of coffee that got them there. Just in case. Maybe love wasn't so blind—or dumb—after all.

They let it cross their palms. They weren't sure if they should be scared or angry or hurt that she thought they might harm her if she showed her hand.

"Aren't you gonna thank me?" she said.

They knew what she wanted. They curled their lips into a sensual sneer. "A-thankya," they said. "A-thankya very much."

She laughed and leaned in and kissed them on the cheek. She turned and vanished into the crowd of bachelor parties and showgirls, bus-trip grannies, and $5 chip dreamers. They unfolded the wad. There was $400. Plenty more where that came from, they were sure. And plenty more to get. She had something better than a poker face. She had a sad glance and a heartbreak smile. She'd do just fine in Vegas.

Skeeter Done Shot Billy Bob

By John M. Floyd

Arlo Hillman leaned forward in his swivel chair, clamped his cigar between his teeth, and stared across his cluttered desk at Sammy Lynch. They were sitting in Arlo's large office in the rear of the Slap Yo Buddy nightclub, along with two other men. Sammy had just entered the room, his face and shirt sweaty from the July heat. The old and noisy air conditioner in the back window was working overtime.

"You mean they shot him?" Arlo asked.

"Sure as hell did," Sammy said, dropping into a chair across from Arlo's desk. "Half hour ago."

"Where?"

"On the fence, while he was trying to climb over it."

"I mean, where bodywise?" Arlo said. "Arm? Shoulder? Back?"

Sammy looked uncomfortable. "Lower."

"What is this, Twenty Questions? Where'd he get shot?"

"Right in his big ass. Dead center."

Arlo frowned. "Seriously?"

"Yep. Just as he was bendin' over the top a' the fence. Hole in one."

Arlo settled back into his squeaky chair and took a moment to think that over. No matter how bad your problems are, he reminded himself, things could always be worse. Then he decided that was wrong. Nothing could be worse than the fix he was in right now. Although, Billy Bob Kelso—the injured party in Sammy's verbal report—might disagree.

As was fitting while engaged in this kind of profound thinking, Arlo pushed his big white cowboy hat back a bit off his forehead. He rarely took it off, indoors or out, and had often been asked if he wore it in the shower. Arlo didn't care. The hat was part of his image, like the cigars.

His mind wandering now, Arlo glanced at the other two people in the room. One was someone he needed: his bookkeeper, Bernard Price. Bernard sat at a giant table counting stacks of cash, stopping occasionally to wave away cigar smoke and write figures in a brown ledger. The second person was someone Arlo didn't need: an overweight slug named Potsy Dalton, who unfortunately happened to be the younger brother of Arlo's wife, Darlene. Potsy was currently glued to the screen of his iPhone, probably playing one of his stupid games. Arlo suspected the skill level was set to FOOL—but even if it was, Potsy was probably losing.

"So, what's the situation at this moment?" Arlo asked, focusing again on Sammy.

"Well, the situation is, he's in the hospital and prob'ly in a lot a pain—"

"Not Billy Bob," Arlo said. "I mean *our* situation. Mine. Them diamonds I stole—"

"*I* stole," Sammy corrected. "As I recall, you sat right here in this office on your fat fanny while *I* used the combination *I* found to get into the jeweler's vault—"

"Okay, the diamonds *we* stole," Arlo said. "The ones that then got stole from *us*, by Calvin Lozano." He shook his head and gnashed his teeth. "That damn Lozano." After calming down a bit, Arlo said, "We're lucky we know exactly where they are."

"You sure you know? You sure we can trust your informant, on this?"

"Yeah. He's one of Lozano's new guards. He knows me from way back, and I can promise you he's too scared of me to lie. The bag a diamonds is sittin' right there on a shelf in the warehouse."

"Lozano's warehouse," Sammy said, as if to underline the problem. "And being watched, apparently, by one of his sharpshooters."

"Only till Lozano gets back in town and can pick 'em up. But, meanwhile—"

Arlo paused and massaged both his temples. "Meanwhile, Benny Belson's gonna come to this office in seven hours and ask me to give the stones to him, and when I tell him I ain't got 'em—"

Sammy gave him a pained look. "Belson eats guys like Cal Lozano for breakfast, Arlo. Why not let Belson's men just steal 'em back?"

"Because it's my responsibility, Sammy. Benny Belson paid *me*—well, me and you—to grab the diamonds 'cause he knew you had a way to get into the jewelry-store safe, and at the moment, Belson knows we stole 'em, but he don't yet know they been stole from *us*, and if I don't have 'em when he comes here tonight, I'll tell you what'll happen then. He—or that damn gorilla that works for him, the biggest of several—will break both a' my legs and then shoot me deader'n a dodo, and you too. You understand that?"

Sammy rubbed his still-damp forehead as if trying to smooth the wrinkles. "I guess."

"Well, I guess you better."

Both of them fell silent. Arlo let out a long breath, settled his hat into place again, low over his eyes like he'd seen John Wayne do once (in *Rio Bravo*, he thought), and studied his other two employees. Across the room, Bernard the Bookkeeper seemed a little nervous at this kind of talk. Potsy Dalton didn't. He probably wasn't even aware of what they were saying. Instead, he looked up from his phone and said, "Hey, Arlo. You got any more a them Snickers bars in your desk drawer?"

Ignoring him, Arlo said to Sammy, "Okay. About the warehouse. Is there any other way in, besides that fence?"

"You know there ain't, Arlo. We already been over this a hundred times. Once we get somebody in, all's well, and the front doors open from the inside. But to *get* in, it's gotta be done the back way, over the fence and through the loading-dock door."

"And you sure we got the right key-code to raise the door?"

"We got the code," Sammy said. "If your contact says the loot's still in there—"

"It's there."

"—then we gotta get over that fence at one certain spot—everyplace else is blocked off. And since somebody done shot Billy Bob while he was tryin' to do exactly that—" Sammy stopped and shook his head. "They wasn't even supposed to know that we know about this back way in, or about the stones bein' in there, neither."

"Okay, shut up for a second," Arlo said. "Let me think." He stewed awhile, puffing like a smokestack, then said, as the idea occurred to him, "You told me there's nothing but an open field on this side a' the fence, right? No cover at all. And you were keepin' a lookout from behind the building down the way, when Billy Bob did his thing. You didn't see nobody out there in the field."

"Not a soul."

"And they didn't shoot you when you went to fetch him when he got shot."

"Well, obviously not," Sammy said. "I'm here, ain't I? They let me run over and drag him out, so I could take him to the hospital."

"So what that means is, they ain't interested in startin' a war. They just want to keep us from gettin' to the diamonds."

Sammy nodded. "Seemed that way to me."

"Well, think about that a minute," Arlo said. "We keep saying 'they,' but we both know it was likely just one guy, and the shooter had to be somewhere on the back side of that open ground. Prob'ly in the woods, right?"

"I figure he musta been. But why go to that trouble? Why not just stay there at the warehouse, pop us from close range?"

"Because then we'd know exactly where the shooter was. Maybe get him first. This kind of thing, we can't defend." Without waiting for agreement, Arlo again lapsed into thought. "How far is that?" he asked. "From the fence to the woods?"

"I dunno. Three hundred yards, maybe four."

"God Almighty. Well, if it's that far away, he's a good shot. A damn good shot." Another pause. "Who do we know, can shoot like that?"

"Nobody 'round here," Sammy said. "Only fella I know of anywhere is Skeeter Tomlinson, and Skeeter's been locked up in a Florida prison three years now. Maybe four."

"You certain about that?"

Sammy shrugged. "I can check."

"Check," Arlo said.

Sammy took out his phone, punched numbers, and leaned back in his chair. As they waited, Potsy Dalton let out a giant belch. Arlo could swear he heard the office windows rattle. Then, seconds later and still playing his video game, Potsy put a hand on his bulging belly and burped again. In the relative silence that followed—Sammy had connected now and was speaking in low tones into his phone—Arlo pointed and said, "Potsy, you do that one more time, and I swear to God, brother-in-law or not, you'll be the next one climbing that fence. Understand?"

"What fence?" Potsy said.

Before Arlo could reply (or pull his gun, which he was strongly considering), Sammy disconnected, looked up, and said, "You were right."

Arlo turned to face him. "What?"

"That was Nate Tully, remember him? Pensacola, a few years back."

"And?"

"Nate said Kieder Tomlinson—that's Skeeter's real name, did you know that?—got outta the pen down there six months ago. In fact, he heard Skeeter might be doing something up this way, right now."

Arlo expelled a long breath. "Great. Here we are, knowing where the golden egg is, and we come to find out Deadeye Dick's settin' out there in the woods with a sniper rifle waitin' to pick us off if we try to climb a nine-foot-tall fence to get to it." He took the cigar from his mouth, scowled at it, and crushed it into an ashtray. "I think we're doing business in the wrong century—I bet Capone or Dillinger never had this kinda trouble."

For a long moment, no one said a word. Then, from the far end of the room, the bookkeeper said, "You believe in coincidences, Arlo?"

All eyes in the room turned to him. "What do you mean, Bernard?"

"I knew Skeeter Tomlinson, too, in the old days. Remember that gal he used to run around with, Gabriella?"

Gabriella. Who could forget? Arlo couldn't recall her last name, but he could sure recall what she looked like and how smitten Skeeter had been, more lovesick than anybody Arlo'd ever seen in his life. And then she'd dumped him, fast and hard. Funny thing was, it didn't seem to matter. Skeeter still mooned over her, day and night. Finally he'd given up and moved to Florida, took some kind of construction job in Tallahassee or some town close to there, just to get away from her and all the bad memories. And, of course, he soon got into trouble. Skeeter always did. Word was, he wound up in Raiford for robbery, serving three to five. Gabriella, Arlo had heard, had relocated also, to someplace up north.

"I remember," Arlo said. "What about her?"

"I saw her today," Bernard said. "Settin' in the bar at the Holiday Inn, the one on Sycamore."

"I'll be damned. I thought she was long gone. Chicago, maybe."

"Don't know nothin' about none a that. I'm just sayin' I saw her. Big as life and good-lookin' as ever."

Arlo squinted, giving that some serious thought. "What were you doing at the Holiday Inn?" he asked.

"Nephew works there, the front desk. You know, my sister Roxie's son. I met him for lunch."

Sammy, listening to all this, said, "Just for the record, Bernard, I'm pretty sure Gabriella's mama still lives here. If she's visiting, why wouldn't she stay with kinfolks?"

"Who knows," Bernard said. "You come see relatives, you don't necessarily bunk there. Besides, I never said she was staying at the motel. I just saw her settin' in the bar."

"Alone?" Sammy asked.

"Yeah. Little table in the corner."

"Well then, she was stayin' there. Who goes to the Holiday Inn bar if they ain't?"

Arlo was losing patience. "Am I missin' something? What the hell's all this got to do with this problem of ours?"

Bernard shrugged. "Nothing, yet. But this Gabriella used to be one a' them jiminy people, you know, jumpin' around, turnin' flips. swingin' from bars—"

"Gymnasts," Arlo said. "She was a gymnast."

"That's it. And well, I got to thinking, Arlo, this big fence that's keeping you from getting back what Lozano took from you? This damn woman we're talkin' about could climb that fence in a split second. And also—"

Suddenly, Arlo understood. "Skeeter wouldn't stop her."

Bernard nodded. "Right. Whether she dumped him or not, hadn't seen him in years or not, she's still Gabriella. Skeeter sees her through that scope. I'm bettin' he couldn't shoot her, even if he knew he had to. Not the way he once felt about her."

Arlo was nodding now, too. Sometimes love, he thought—even if it's one-way—never dies.

The room had gone quiet except for the occasional beep and ding from whatever game Arlo's nitwit brother-in-law was playing. But Arlo's mind was racing. The bookkeeper's suggestion sounded crazy, but Arlo had a feeling it would take something crazy to get him and his buddies out of this mess.

Still looking at Bernard, he said, "How much you think should we offer her?"

"Assuming we can find her—"

"We'll find her," Arlo said. "I agree with Sammy—she's got a room at the motel."

"In that case..." Bernard frowned, thinking. "I'd start with ten thousand and take it up to twenty if you had to. Them diamonds are worth fifty times that."

Arlo looked at Sammy Lynch. "Think she'd do it?"

Sammy shrugged. "Can't hurt to ask."

* * *

They went through Bernard's nephew Jeff at the motel to locate her. None of them could give him a last name, but Jeff said no problem, there was only one Gabriella registered, and ten seconds later, sure enough, he connected Arlo to the phone in her room. The pitch Arlo made to her turned out sounding less awkward and strange than he'd thought it would, and when she heard his abridged version of what he needed her to do and how much he would pay her for doing it and that the decision had to be made right *now*, she amazed him by agreeing on the spot. Twenty minutes after Arlo spoke with her on the phone, she was standing beside him and Sammy in the private office behind the Slap Yo Buddy. Skeeter's name was never mentioned by anyone, and around four o'clock that afternoon—five hours before Arlo was scheduled to turn the missing merchandise over to Benny Belson or die what he suspected would be a painful and humiliating death—Gabriella left with Sammy for the warehouse. Or, more accurately, for the vantage point thirty yards from the spot in the warehouse fence where Billy Bob Kelso had earlier that day taken a bullet to the hindquarters for his fellow thugs.

Arlo stayed behind, along with Bernard, who was still fiddling with the past week's proceeds from both the bar and their other activities, and Potsy, who was snoring in his chair with his mouth hanging open like a trapdoor. Arlo found himself wishing he had a spoonful of rat poison handy.

Mostly, though, he thought about other things, like the unpleasant fact that the shooter might not be Skeeter Tomlinson at all. If it *was* Skeeter—and Arlo was pretty sure it was—Gabriella would almost certainly sail past with flying colors and then make her exit from the building on the other side, where Sammy would be waiting to pick her up and bring her safely back to the office, along with the diamonds—at which point she would happily be paid the agreed sum of fifteen thousand bucks and given a sincere thank-you and a fond farewell. But if it *wasn't* Skeeter...well, that was another story. Gabriella wouldn't make it past the fence, they'd have another casualty to haul off, and the diamonds would stay where they were. And Arlo Hillman would have to decide whether to take his chances with Cal Lozano and his apes tonight at nine or pack up and run for the hills and keep running. He hoped fervently—for both his sake and Gabriella's—that wouldn't be the case.

At any rate, Gabriella had been told about none of this. All she knew was the route she was supposed to take and what she was supposed to do when she got past the fence and loading dock and into the building and then get out again. She had *not* been told what was in the bag she was after and, in fact, had been instructed not to even open it and look inside, in case it was boobytrapped. The bullshit level was halfway up the wall by this time, but somehow Gabriella didn't seem to suspect anything. All Arlo could do was pray to God, and cross his fingers and toes, and hope for the best.

At 4:25 Sammy phoned him from the scene. Gabriella was over the fence and inside the warehouse. All was well. Arlo felt a surge of blessed relief.

Then, at a quarter to five, Sammy called again, this time from the warehouse parking lot. He'd been watching the front doors like a hungry eagle for the past twenty minutes, he said, and there was no sign of Gabriella. When Arlo's heart started beating again, he ordered Sammy to go back to his spot near the back fence, quick, and take a look around; maybe she'd misunderstood and retraced her steps after grabbing the loot. Arlo hoped not. He hadn't wanted whoever was watching from the woods to see her come back out that way. If that happened, Skeeter the Shooter might have a sudden and unexpected change of heart and be tempted to stop her—or Sammy—before they could get away. Maybe shoot the tires out on their car, if they made it that far, or maybe even kill Gabriella outright, in spite of the fact Arlo had figured he wouldn't.

Now, though, he didn't know *what* to think.

Sammy called again, from the hiding place behind the buildings near the fence, and said he saw nothing there either. Arlo was well aware that there'd probably been enough time, now, for their hired gymnast to have grabbed the goods, doubled back, and climbed the fence, and gone anywhere in the world from there. The fact that she wasn't lying dead in plain sight re-confirmed Arlo's certainty that the marksman was Skeeter Tomlinson. But at this point, that was little consolation.

Again, Sammy went around front. Still no Gabriella.

Arlo, sweating and desperate by this time, told Bernard to call the motel and ask his nephew—Jeff?—whether she had come back there, and, if not, tell him to keep an eye open for her. If she did show up there, Sammy could head that way, find her, and recover the diamonds. But if she'd doublecrossed them—maybe she'd looked inside the bag after all, warnings or not (and that possibility was becoming more likely with every passing minute)—would she even *go* back to the motel?

Before Bernard disconnected, Arlo had a thought. He hopped up, crossed the room, and motioned to Bernard to hand over his phone.

"Jeff?" Arlo said into it, and identified himself. "Is there any way our friend Gabriella could get up to her room without your seeing her?"

"No, sir. She's in Room Five-Fourteen. I know what she looks like, and I can see both sets of elevators from here."

"What if she takes the stairs instead?"

A pause. "Oh. Well, I suppose she could do that..."

Arlo turned to Bernard. "Call Sammy on the landline, quick. Send him to the motel, but tell him to go up and wait outside her room. Five-Fourteen." Then Arlo said into the phone, as the thought occurred to him, "One more question, Jeff. Is Gabriella the only one registered for that room?"

"Let's see..."

Arlo waited.

"No," Jeff said. "It's Mrs. Tomlinson *and* her husband."

Arlo blinked. "What?"

"Double occupancy. Kieder and Gabriella Tomlinson."

Arlo froze, and swallowed hard. He felt his knees go weak. When his muscles unlocked, he disconnected and stumbled back to his desk. Without a word to anyone he sagged into his chair, took off his hat, and ran a trembling hand through his hair. Bernard, watching him, said, "Arlo? You okay?" Then, into the landline phone: "Hold on, Sammy. Something's up."

Dazedly, Arlo looked at Bernard. "Tell Sammy to come back here, fast. Tell him Gabriella won't be going back to the room. Neither of them will."

"What do you mean, neither of them?" Bernard asked. He had taken the phone from his ear, and looked lost.

Arlo knew the feeling. He was staring now at the summer afternoon sky outside the window, wishing he were anywhere in the whole wide world but here inside this office. *Skeeter and Gabriella*, he thought. *Sometimes, love never dies.*

"Start packing our stuff," he said to Bernard. "We're leaving."

"What?"

"Tell Sammy we gotta be gone, outta here, far from here, before nine o'clock tonight," Arlo said, his eyes still on the window. "He'll understand."

Potsy Dalton, lying on the couch near the back wall, looked up from his video game. "We goin' someplace?" he asked and belched.

"*We* are," Arlo said. "You can stay."

The Collar

By Carolina Garcia-Aguilera

Havana, June 1961

"Mariana, did you hear the news?" My friend Lourdes whispered, sitting next to me on a bench, as we were lacing up our pointe shoes in the ballerina's dressing room of the Gran Teatro of Havana. The morning rehearsal for *Giselle* was starting in a few minutes, so there wasn't much time to talk. "Wonderful news!

"What news?" I looked around to make sure we weren't being overheard. Spies were everywhere in Fidel Castro's Cuba, and any one of our fellow dancers would be more than happy to denounce us as counterrevolutionary—especially if it meant taking our place in the *corps de ballet*. "And keep your voice down!"

"It's Nureyev! Your hero, Rudolph Nureyev!" Lourdes could barely sit still. "He defected! He was in the bathroom at Le Bourget Airport in Paris, and he got away from his Soviet minders and asked for asylum!"

I was so surprised that I dropped my shoe. "Nureyev defected?" I could barely believe it. Rudolph Nureyev was one of the best—if not the best—male ballet dancers in the world. His story was a well-known one: a soloist in the renowned Kirov Opera when he became a star at the age of twenty. Soon after, he went from one of Russia's most famous dancers to a worldwide star.

Lourdes looked around. "My cousin Lydia—you remember her, she works

65

at the French embassy—she told me this morning. She knows about it because it happened in France."

"I can't believe it," I said.

Lourdes took my right hand and squeezed it as she whispered. "Nureyev was on tour in Paris with the Kirov ballet and was about to board a flight to London with the rest of the company when he was told he had to go back to Moscow."

"Tell me everything." I inched closer to her on the bench. We were alone in the dressing room, but one could never assume they were safe.

Lourdes took a deep breath. "It sounds like Nureyev was suspicious about being called back to Russia in the middle of the tour," she reported. "He's apparently very rebellious, and the Soviets were getting suspicious about how much he's been mixing with Westerners. He might have gone home and gotten thrown in prison. The only reason they let him out of Russia was so the world would know the Soviets are the premier country for ballet, but they had KGB deputies watching him day and night."

"So, what happened? Where is he now?" Lourdes and I would be late joining the other dancers for rehearsal, but I didn't care. I had been in love with Nureyev for years and followed his career like an obsession. My greatest dream was to dance with him.

Although I was a member of the *corps de ballet*, our director had told me that she was considering making me a soloist. She should have elevated me to that position years before—I worked hard and was considered the most talented dancer—but she had suspicions about my enthusiasm (or lack of) for how the Cuban National Ballet was run. And so, I had languished.

Mostly I disagreed with how political the company had become, no great surprise since Fidel Castro himself was responsible for its existence and gave it a substantial state subsidy for operations. Law 812 had passed in 1959, obliging the government to support and defend ballet while giving the Ministry of Education responsibility and oversight over it. As a result, we had a bunch of bureaucrats—mainly militia types who didn't know a *jete* from a *pas de deux*—dictating to us and constantly interfering.

However, the director had changed her attitude toward me when it became known that I had become the *protégé* of Miguel Martinez-Mendoza. Miguel was the Minister of Public Works and a very powerful man in Castro's circle who would be very dangerous to cross. The director knew how to look after her own career and had no interest in professional suicide, so she knew keeping me happy meant keeping her job—and perhaps even her freedom. The promotion was just a matter of time.

Lourdes peered around to make sure we were alone before speaking again. "Look, Mariana, I'll tell you more after rehearsal. Let's meet at the Parque Central."

"Agreed. I can't wait to hear how he did it."

Rehearsal seemed to take forever. We didn't even really need it—the company had been performing *Giselle* for the last two years. But questioning directives from the top was risky, so we all plastered smiles on our faces and rehearsed a ballet we could dance in our sleep.

Lourdes Rodriguez and I had been friends since first grade, and we trusted one another completely. We agreed on how much we disliked how the Cuban Nacional Ballet was run, but Lourdes was willing to envision her entire future with the *Corps de Ballet* there while I was more ambitious. She knew about my unhappiness and often cautioned me to keep my mouth shut.

Lourdes' brother, Luis, was a photographer and a friend of my brother Ernesto, so I had known him pretty much my whole life as well. We had flirted when we were younger, but nothing ever came of it. Luis worked for the Ministry of Tourism, and he was as unhappy as I was with life under the Castro regime. When we knew no one was listening, we often talked about how much we both wanted to leave the island and go to the United States. Luis wanted to be a portrait photographer in America, knowing there was only so much he could accomplish at home on the island.

Lourdes was late in leaving the rehearsal, so I waited for her in the park. It was the public place in Havana I liked best and one of the few the government hadn't screwed up with their "reforms." The Parque Central in the heart of old Havana was cozy and verdant, with a statue of Jose Marti—the patriot-poet hero of Cuba—at its center. That statue had been erected in 1905 and was surrounded by twenty-eight majestic palms. I often came there during breaks and just gazed at it. I wondered what Jose Marti, the champion of freedom, would think about life under the Castro regime. The revolution had promised to end poverty on the island, but instead, people were becoming poorer.

Finally, Lourdes came out of the Gran Teatro. I looked up and marveled at what a beautiful building it was, with its neo-Gothic pillars, arches, and ornate sculptures. No matter how disillusioned with the frustrations and blocks I encountered there, I knew I was fortunate to dance in such a majestic place.

Lourdes joined me on the bench, and I started peppering her with questions. "What happened? How did Nureyev defect? How did he get away?"

"Mariana, let me catch my breath." Lourdes sat close next to me. "This is what I know. Lydia told me that Nureyev was in Paris at a reception honoring French and Russian dancers. He made friends with the French dancers, going out with them to Parisian restaurants, theaters, and clubs. Of course, he was always followed by the KGB. Finally, his minders had enough and ordered him back to Moscow. That was when he made his move. At the airport, he threw himself at the mercy of two French policemen just before he was supposed to board the flight to Moscow. Because they were in France, there was nothing the Russians could do!"

Lourdes' eyes shone with excitement, and I felt a flush of inspiration. Nureyev and I came from different worlds, but there were similarities in our lives. His defection meant he decided he could no longer live and reach his artistic potential under an oppressive regime. I knew I wasn't at his level, but I also knew we both needed to live in freedom.

I couldn't remember when ballet wasn't at the center of my life. I enrolled in the Ballet in 1955, when it was established under the legendary *prima ballerina* Alicia Alonso. Alicia and her husband Fernando were friends of Fidel Castro and were both fervent supporters of the Revolution. The Cuban Nacional Ballet was so under the thrall of the revolution that the dancers were called *guerrilleras* and performed in factories and sugar cane fields. They even hurt themselves joining in the harvest.

The ballet flourished in Cuba under Alicia Alonso, becoming a world-class company with wonderful dancers. Alicia ran the ballet with an iron fist, never tolerating a hint of dissenting opinions. No dancer would be able to advance at the company without her approval, and only those who displayed sufficient allegiance were allowed to leave the country on tour. I had never traveled abroad, but I kept up on the news outside our island as best as I could—especially about the ballet world.

I was twenty-two, and I had reached my caliber as a dancer because of the training I received at the Cuban Nacional Ballet. But I yearned to chart the course of my own life, and my art, without the government telling me what to do every step of the way. I was grateful to the company, but I wanted artistic freedom to dance what I wanted with the partners of my choosing. None of that was going to happen if I stayed in Havana.

I had grown up in a small two-story house in the Miramar district of the city. Along with my parents, I had two older brothers and a younger sister. My father was a pharmacist, while my mother stayed at home. None of our family ever had anything to do with the ballet world, but when I was a young child, I used to play with my neighbor Teresa at her house, and her mother, Irina, was a ballerina with Alicia Alonso's company.

Irina had transformed one of the bedrooms in her family's house into a dance studio, and I would watch and imitate her movements as she practiced. It was soon obvious that I had talent, so Irina took me to Alicia for an introduction. I performed some exercises as Alicia watched and was immediately accepted into the company. It was a tough, rigorous apprenticeship, but I completed it. I really loved being a dancer at the company until the Revolution came, but then everything changed. The easy, free feel of our days was gone. Alicia Alonso became a functionary of the government.

I'd been with the company for five years when my life took a sudden turn because Miguel came into my life. He had seen me dance *Swan Lake* two years before and asked for an introduction. I knew I stood out from the other dancers in the *corps* with my curves and rather large breasts; the others were mostly flat-chested waifs. Of course, the ballet director understood Miguel's intentions toward me but agreed anyway—no one would refuse a man as important as him. I had no other choice but to become his mistress at the age of twenty unless I wanted to lose my place in the Cuban Nacional Ballet and be blackballed from dancing forever.

Miguel was fifty and married with six children. He set me up in a luxurious apartment in El Vedado that had been confiscated from a family that fled to Miami. The apartment's occupants had left so quickly that it was still full of their furniture, art, and personal belongings. Sometimes, at night, when I couldn't sleep, I would carefully look at their photos in silver frames in every room and wonder how their new lives were going away from Cuba. I was torn between feeling sad for them leaving everything behind and happy and jealous they were living in freedom.

Miguel was very generous. He gave me money for my family, and they accepted the arrangement. My lover was very ordinary looking, of average height and weight with washed out yellowish eyes and thinning dark brown hair. Thankfully he kept his face clean shaven, without the scruffy beard of the militia men who had fought with Castro in the Sierra Maestra, the mountains in western Cuba where Castro had launched the Revolution. He also wore a *guayabera* and linen pants instead of green army fatigues.

As a trusted friend, Miguel had been with Castro for years. First, he had been the Revolution's accountant, then he moved up to Minister of Public Works, a position that give him a license to steal. And he joyfully did. I didn't object to that since I was the beneficiary of his largesse. When it became known that I was his mistress, I was treated with the kind of false respect (and fear) that came with the position.

Becoming an older man's mistress at the age of twenty hadn't been my goal in life. Miguel claimed his wife denied him sex, but I doubted it—in addition to the six children they already had, a seventh was on the way. What I think she denied him was what he had a passion for: kinky sex, especially role-playing and bondage.

It bothered me in the beginning, but I got used to it as time passed, and I went along to keep him happy. I didn't care for it when he would dress me up in olive green fatigues and a militia man's cap and have me point an (unloaded) gun in his direction while he entered me from behind. He also liked to take full advantage of the extreme positions I could achieve with my ballerina's flexibility, seeming to find it very satisfying.

The night Lourdes told me about Nureyev's defection, I had a very vivid dream in which he and I were dancing *Giselle* with me in the title role and him as Prince Albrecht. *Giselle* was a tragic romantic ballet in two acts, with Giselle as a peasant girl and Albrecht as a nobleman disguised as a peasant. The ballet ends in heartbreak when Giselle learns that her love Albrecht is engaged to marry a princess, and she dies of sadness. It's a demanding role for a *prima ballerina*, requiring a lot of strength and stamina.

Traditionally, male ballet dancers served in supporting roles to the ballerinas. But Nureyev, with his strength and power, became equal in the spotlight. I was confident that with him as my partner, we could dance *Giselle* together and take with ballet world by storm. That night was when I started to plan how to leave Cuba, so I could dance with Rudi.

I didn't know how I was going to defect, but I also knew I didn't want to be penniless in my new life. There was one other thing: I was going to take my dog with me into exile. When Miguel first set me up, he saw that I was unhappy and had given me a large poodle that I named Pirouette. She was my constant companion. She slept on my bed, which offended Miguel—an oddly delicate reaction, I thought, given his personal preferences. It was true that Pirouette wasn't exactly easy to love—she was very big, with black hair that shed everyplace, and she often drooled and barked into thin air. But I did.

Every time Miguel made a new and weird sexual demand, he would compensate by giving me a piece of jewelry. There was a kind of consistent logic to it. The more perverted and, sometimes, more dangerous Miguel's requirements became, the more expensive the jewels he gave me afterwards. After one particularly debauched session, he gave me a five-carat diamond. Knowing what was coming my way afterwards, I agreed to whatever he asked. I would shut my eyes and, instead of acknowledging what was happening, imagine myself dancing as a *prima ballerina* with the exquisite Nureyev as my partner.

Miguel came from an unsophisticated background and a family of farmers, but he had surprisingly fine taste in jewelry. I suspected the gifts he gave me had been stolen or been given to him as bribes by individuals desperate for his help or patronage. Since I didn't have anything to do with Miguel's business, I accepted his gifts with no questions asked. I kept them in a small closet where I stored Pirouette's food and toys and blankets, knowing Miguel would never go prying around there.

When I thought about how I was going to leave Cuba with Pirouette, one idea kept coming to me: that it was going to start with my sex life with Miguel.

We were lying in bed together, relaxing after a particularly vigorous, debauched session, when I decided it was time to broach the subject. Miguel was a very intelligent man, with a suspicious nature verging on paranoia, so I knew I would pay dearly if he suspected I had ulterior motives. Still, I had to take the risk.

"Miguel, *querido*. You know how much I like it when we play act." I began.

Miguel nodded, with his eyes closed. "Yes, Mariana, that's part of what makes us so special." He opened one eye and looked at me. "You enjoy it too, right?"

"Of course, Miguel, I enjoy it very much." I let out a theatrical sigh. "But maybe, just for some variety to spice things up, you might consider being the one in bondage?"

Miguel shot up in bed as though I'd pointed a (loaded) gun at him. "You think? I feel that having you as the one in bondage is quite satisfying."

I started to stroke him the way he liked. "Never mind. It was just a thought. A way to make things even more...satisfying." I left it at that. I knew Miguel well enough to be sure the idea would stick in his head. I had planted a seed, and I had to be patient and allow it to grow.

Sure enough, it was less than a week before he brought it up again when we were lying in bed together, having exhausted one another.

"Mariana, remember when you said it would be exciting for me to be the one tied up?" He smiled. "I thought about it, and I think it's a good idea."

He got up and walked naked toward the chair by the window, where he had left a bag when he came in earlier. He picked it up and brought it to the bed.

"I came prepared." With a sly expression, Miguel began to lay out some things on the bed for me to admire. It was bondage gear—in his size.

I mustered as much enthusiasm as I could. I didn't relish what lay ahead, but at least that part of my plan was working. We agreed to try it the next time we were together. Miguel found it difficult to get free, between his work and family obligations, and he usually came to my apartment in the late afternoon, three or four days a week for a couple of hours at a time. My time was also highly scheduled with rehearsals and performances, along with the social obligations that came with being part of the ballet company.

I had a window for leaving Cuba legally, but it was closing quickly. The disastrous Bay of Pigs Invasion had just happened in April, when Cuban exiles backed by the United States had launched an invasion of the island and been soundly defeated. That had culminated in Castro pulling into a closer relationship with the Soviet Union and declaring himself a Marxist-Leninist. Relations between Cuba and America were officially severed when Cuba nationalized the U.S. and other foreign properties and the Americans closed their embassy. As far as immigration was concerned, the situation was dire. Previously, the American government would issue visas for Cubans who wanted to leave, but all of that had changed. Visas were now doled out only for humanitarian reasons, for Cubans who could claim that they faced oppression from the communist regime on the island. Thousands of Cubans, disillusioned with the Castro regime, had left, with most going to Miami, but that loophole was closing.

It wasn't just the visa situation that was changing fast. The Revolution was accelerating. All aspects of Cuban life were starting to belong entirely to the government. Private schools were seized, and all education was nationalized under government control. Even worse, personal bank accounts were being taken over. Pretty soon, no one would be able to leave.

Because Miguel was so important and close to the regime, he had the kind of power that only a handful of individuals did. He would often brag to me that he could get things accomplished that few others could. One of the strings he was able to pull was obtaining American visas for powerful people, despite the growing rift between the two countries. That detail had certainly stood out amidst all his boasting.

And he had done other good things for me. Miguel had tipped me off just before the government nationalized private bank accounts. As a result, I had been able to close my bank account and keep my money stored with the jewels and the dog food. I saw life in Cuba becoming more difficult for everyone around me who wasn't an insider with the regime. Personal freedoms were disappearing by the day. And my time felt increasingly borrowed, dependent on staying in Miguel's favor.

Miguel wasn't really a bad man. Apart from his weird sexual demands, he could be kind and generous. He was an important man in a scary world, and I needed his protection. If that meant I had to do physically repulsive things to leave Cuba, then I would. Continuing to dance in the Cuban Nacional Ballet was going to mean never dancing with Nureyev or seeing the world the way I wanted.

Thanks to Miguel, I knew a little secret about El Comandante. Fidel Castro might have loved women and had many lovers, in addition to being married with an unknown number of children, but he was also a bit of a prude. This didn't stop him from having affairs, but he didn't like that kind of reputation spreading around. He wanted to be known as a family man.

Because Miguel had known Fidel for many years, he had often told me stories of Fidel's hypocrisy. The man presented one face to the world and another in his private life. This was the double standard that was going to get me out of Cuba.

I went to visit my father at the pharmacy where he worked. He was the head pharmacist at the Drogueria Suarez on the corner of Galliano and San Rafael Streets in an old part of Havana. I used to love visiting him there when I was a child, fascinated by the large, brightly colored glass jars filled with mysterious liquids lining the walls. My father had worked there for more than twenty years, and he was well-liked and respected, one of the reasons many regular customers visited the place—and why the government left him alone.

"*Hola* Papi!" I called out as I entered the store. I went behind the counter, where he was filling a prescription, and hugged him tightly. "How are you? Working too much like always?"

"Mariana, my child, you look beautiful as usual." He kissed me in greeting. "What brings you here to see me?" Papi led me to the sitting area in the back of the store, where we sat down next to one another on a narrow old sofa.

"To see you, of course," I replied. "But also, to ask for something."

I hated to be using Papi for my own ends, but I really had no other choice given the plan I had set in motion. My heart lurched in my chest when I realized this might be the last time that I would see him before leaving.

"Of course, my child. Anything you need." Papi looked at me with such a sweet expression, the same one he'd given me when I was a little girl, that I almost broke out in tears.

I took a long breath and looked into his eyes. "I'm having trouble sleeping." I cursed myself for lying to him. "And I need to be well rested to perform my best. I can't be tired when I'm on my feet all day."

"You need something to help you sleep?" He asked, with concern in his voice.

I nodded. "Exactly." I looked beseechingly at him. "Do you have something that can help me get to sleep—quickly and deeply?"

"Oh yes, I have just the thing to help you." Papi got up and disappeared into the pharmacy. He came back a few minutes later holding a small, clear bag containing about an inch of white powder. He handed it over carefully.

"This will help, Mariana, but be careful. It's very strong. Put one small teaspoon in water or any other liquid and stir it well. You'll feel very drowsy in a couple of minutes, and then you'll fall into a deep sleep. But drink it when you're already lying down. The effects come on fast, and I don't want you falling and hurting yourself."

I stood up and thanked my father, hugging him tightly as I blinked back tears. It was painful to think this could be the last time I ever saw him, or the *drogueria* where I had spent so much of my childhood.

"I'll let you know how it goes." I kissed him and took in his familiar scent, savoring this last moment.

I slowly walked back to the apartment, thinking of everything that I would be leaving behind in Cuba if my plan worked. I wasn't wavering in my choice to defect, with all the danger it represented, but it wasn't easy to leave my beloved home, even if it meant dancing with Nureyev one day. With each step forward, I realized how precarious the coming days would be for me. But I would risk jail to dance with Rudi.

Back at the apartment, the afternoon light streamed through the gaps in the shutters. *"Amor,* do you want another drink before we get started?" I smiled sweetly at Miguel and held out a glass filled to the rim with his favorite Johnny Walker Red.

We were both dressed, or semi-dressed, in our bondage gear and had just finished one awkward session. Miguel had been thrilled and was ready to go for another. He looked ridiculous in leather straps, but I gave him my most sultry look.

"Gracias." Miguel accepted the glass and took a long drink. I had stirred a heaping teaspoon of the sleeping potion into it when he had been lying in post-sexual bliss. The extra dose, along with the alcohol, had to do the job. If he were to wake up during what I intended to do, I surely would end up in front of a firing squad.

I watched Miguel drain half the glass, then the rest. Less than a minute later, his head fell silently to the bed sheets, and he was out cold. I took the glass to the kitchen to thoroughly wash it and to eliminate any trace of what it had contained.

When I got back to the bedroom, I found Miguel unresponsive, completely still, his breathing shallow. I almost panicked, thinking for a second that I had killed him, but I heard a long snore-like rattle and saw his chest rise and fall. I quickly went to the cabinet where I kept Pirouette's things and took out my camera. I made sure the film was correctly installed and returned to the bedroom. Miguel was in the same position as I'd left him. He looked totally ridiculous, in a neck collar, blindfolded, with black leather locking cuffs and a red rubber ball gag that I placed carefully into his mouth. He was otherwise naked.

After confirming he was still breathing, I climbed up on the bed so I could take pictures of him, in that pose, from above. I snapped a few and removed the blindfold from his eyes. I needed him to be as identifiable as possible. Then, I carefully shifted him to the center of the bed into a spread-eagle position. I took the other black leather locking cuffs on his wrists and ankles from the bedroom restraining kit in his bag and re-tied him. I took some more photos. After that, I rolled him over onto his belly and took some more pictures with a spanking paddle lying next to his neck collar. Might as well be artistic, I thought.

Moving Miguel around, I silently thanked my ballet teachers for all the many exercises they'd made us repeat over and over. Although I had cursed them at the time, they had made me strong. By the time I was done, I had taken a total of about twenty photographs.

Papi hadn't told me how long the sleeping powder would last, so I didn't know how much more time I had before Miguel woke up. I had given him a big dose, so it should have been a while. I had to hope it didn't kill him.

I decided to strip him out of the bondage gear and slip him into his underwear so he would be more comfortable. I returned the gear to the bag and waited, watching the lengthening shadows on the wall.

When he woke up a couple of hours later, he was startled, looking around confused. "What happened?"

"*Amor*, you fell into such a deep sleep. I think I wore you out. I took you out of the bondage gear because I didn't want it to leave any marks while you were unconscious." I explained.

He stared at me, then gave me a little grin. "Maybe we wore each other out. But next time, we'll last longer."

"Of course, *Amor*." I gave him a naughty smile. "We've only just begun to explore."

Before he left, Miguel gently pressed a small box in my hands. I could barely wait to open it. New adventures, after all, meant fancier rewards.

Less than a minute after Miguel left, I headed to Pirouette's cabinet, found the box where I had hidden the jewelry that he had given me during the past two years, tucked away in there, and carried it over to the bed. I took out the pieces of jewelry and lined them up left to right from least valuable to most. I also thought of everything I had done to earn them. I had amassed a small fortune.

I went to the kitchen and returned with my sharpest knife. Sitting on the edge of the bed, I slowly and methodically cut each stone from its setting. By the time I was done, I counted twenty-six stones: fourteen diamonds, ten square cut, and four round, along with three emeralds, five rubies, and four pearls. I had no idea what it was all worth, but I knew they would get me started on my new life.

I slowly stroked Pirouette as I ran over options in my mind as to how to get the stones out of Cuba. I was determined not to leave the island penniless. It was very much against the law to try to smuggle anything of value off the island. The punishment if caught was a long term in prison—and the government would make my family suffer as well. It was a huge risk. Pirouette sensed my anxiety and started licking my hand to comfort me.

Looking down at her dark eyes, it was like a lightning bolt had hit me. I had just figured how I was going to get out of Cuba with my dog and my stones.

Early the next morning, I telephoned Lourdes's brother Luis and asked if he would meet me at the Parque Central. I had rehearsals all day, so it was late afternoon before I was able to get there. Luis was waiting for me when I arrived.

"Hola, Luis," I greeted him. "How are you?"

Luis shook his head. "*Ay*, Mariana, not so good. It's working for the government. My boss has me spending all day photographing scenes that show the 'glory' of the Revolution and the greatness of Fidel and how much the people love him."

"That doesn't sound easy," I commented.

Luis looked so sad that I almost hugged him. "I just can't do it anymore, Mariana. Fidel is ruining this country. I'm worried all the time that I'm going to do something or say something that's going to land me in jail—or worse. And then what's going to happen to my family?"

Thankfully, there was no one else in earshot. "I understand, Luis. I'm in the same situation as you."

I thought about the old saying: *Man plans, God laughs*. It certainly applied to me that afternoon. The ballet director had pulled me aside after rehearsal and told me that next month, I would be dancing a solo—I was getting promoted out of the *corps*. I had been waiting for this for more than a year, and so I put on an act of thanking her profusely, thinking that by the time my big moment arrived, I would be far away. Or in prison.

While I was still standing there listening to her, the thought had hit me: why was this happening while I was on the verge of defecting? Did they know? Was I being set up for a trap? No one could be paranoid enough in those days in Castro's Cuba, when anything was possible.

"So, Mariana, why did you want to meet?" Luis looked searchingly at me. "Not that I don't enjoy seeing you, but you made it sound urgent."

I reached into the bag where I kept my ballet clothes and shoes and, after looking around one more time to make sure no one seemed to be watching, I handed Luis the roll of film I'd shot the day before.

"This could be very dangerous for both of us," I told him. "But I need your help."

Luis calmly took the roll and placed it in his shoulder bag. "What do you need, Mariana, that's so dangerous?"

I lowered my voice. "I need that roll of film developed. It contains very incriminating photos of my patron, Miguel. You know he's a powerful man. If you don't want to take such a risk, then just tell me, and I'll find another way."

Luis thought for a moment. I was asking him to take a chance, but I was also taking one myself. If Miguel learned what I had done, my life would be finished.

Finally, Luis nodded. "I'll do anything to screw with those bastards. I hate them all so much, I'm happy to do something to hurt one of them. Let me get started tonight. I'll have them developed for you tomorrow."

I put my hand on his shoulder. "Thank you so much, Luis. You are wonderful to help me."

I sat on a bench and watched Luis walking away until I couldn't see him any longer. Then, clutching my bag close, I walked until I arrived at a store that sold things for pets, not the usual one I frequented for Pirouette's things. As

I scanned the shelves, I thought how fortunate it was that Miguel was away that evening attending a meeting for Castro's ministers. It was important that he didn't visit me that night. I had many things to do.

As he had promised, Luis delivered the photos to me the next afternoon. They came out even better than I had hoped. Luis stood silently as I looked through the small folder of pictures. I felt a flash of embarrassment as I looked at Miguel in his bondage outfit. It was humiliating, having Luis get a glimpse of the things I'd done. The photos deepened my resolve to get out of Cuba with a clean, new start on life.

"Mariana, I don't know what you plan to do with those pictures, but I want to wish you luck." Luis nodded at the folder. "One thing I can see is that you're playing a very dangerous game. Please be very careful. He's very powerful and could cause a lot of harm. You know that, right?"

"I know." I looked into his eyes. "But I must get out of here. I need to dance in freedom."

He smiled. "Your beloved Nureyev, right?" He took my hand. "I hope it comes true for you, Mariana. You're a wonderful dancer. You deserve to be on the greatest stages. But how do you plan to leave? The Americans aren't issuing visas anymore. They closed the embassy."

"It's best you don't know too many details," I told him.

Luis and I hugged goodbye and went our separate ways. I headed to my parents' home to spend the evening with them. They were surprised, because I hadn't stopped by in a while, but they were pleased when I said I just wanted to spend time at home. I tried to be cheerful and upbeat during the few hours that I was there, but it was difficult. Tears kept welling in my eyes.

The next day Miguel said he would be coming by in the afternoon, so I prepared for his visit. I was both excited and frightened by what I planned to say and do, but I wasn't about to back out. I knew how furious he was going to be, and so I had packed what few belongings I planned to take with me. And I made sure that Pirouette was ready.

I had a glass filled with Johnny Walker Red waiting for him. Miguel was pleased and, anticipating a sexy afternoon, he smiled and kissed me.

"What a pleasant surprise, Mariana." He took the glass and drank half of it in a single gulp. He started to undress, motioning with a nod toward the bedroom.

"Not just yet, Miguel." I stayed where I was. "I need to speak with you about something important."

I saw the annoyance on Miguel's features. Knowing his arrogance, he probably thought I wanted something crazy, like for him to leave his wife and marry me.

"What is it?" His tie was in his hand. "What's so important?"

"Let's sit." I patted the seat next to me on the sofa and watched Miguel reluctantly lower himself down next to me. "You and I have been in a relationship for just more than two years now."

He looked perplexed, but he nodded.

"Miguel, I've told you many times about my ambition to leave Cuba and perform with an international ballet company."

Miguel frowned. "The Cuban Nacional Ballet is an outstanding company. Alicia Alonso has made it first-rate, and you've done very well there." He shook his head. "Why would you want to dance with another company? You're rising there. The director told me she's going to promote you to soloist."

I thought about what Miguel had just revealed. I had only learned I was being promoted the day before. It confirmed, yet again, how everything had become political. Did I deserve to be soloist, or was I getting it because of Miguel? It didn't matter. Miguel couldn't get me a spot with Nureyev—that was mine to earn alone.

"That's true, Miguel, but I want to go to America. And I want to leave now."

Miguel looked as though I had physically hit him. "I don't understand, Mariana. You dance with a world-famous company. You live in a beautiful apartment. I give you everything you want. I give you jewelry. I even got you that wretched dog. What the hell else do you need?"

I looked him straight in the eyes. "Freedom, Miguel. That's what I need."

He scoffed at my words. "The Revolution gives everyone freedom. This is paradise. Why would you reject the wonder that Cuba has become?"

Miguel's reaction was far from unexpected. I needed to tread very carefully now to avoid staring at the walls of a prison cell or worse.

"I'm very grateful to you, *Amor*," I told him. "You have been so very generous with me. You've treated me like a princess. I know it, and I thank you."

"Then why would you want to leave?" Miguel's eyes narrowed. "Are you against the Revolution, Mariana? Because if you are, you know what that means."

"No, no, Miguel. Life in Cuba is perfect." I made my voice soothing and sincere. "I must leave, though, for my career. I want to dance in other companies. There are things that I can't do if I stay here."

"You're not leaving Cuba." His mouth was set in a hard, straight line. "You're not leaving me. I'll stop you. I'll have you thrown in jail."

He got up, instantly furious, yelling. "I can do it, and I will." He walked over to the telephone. "I'm making the call right now."

I had little doubt that he would do as he said. If I became too much trouble, he wouldn't find it difficult to replace me. So, I reached for the manila envelope on the coffee table.

"Before you make that call, look at these."

I opened the envelope and took out the photos of him in my bed, naked except for the bondage gear. I stepped back as Miguel carefully inspected the twenty-plus highly focused and expertly developed pictures.

The fury in his eyes made my blood run cold.

"You bitch." He snarled. "You whore. How could you?"

I smiled sweetly. "There are copies of all of these in a safe place."

His chin jutted out, but then he seemed to think for a moment, and he collapsed back down to the sofa and accepted the inevitable. "What do you want, Mariana?"

Miguel knew well what would happen to him if those photos were made public. His career would be finished. He would be ruined; the bribes and the money he constantly stole and skimmed would be gone, along with his power over other people. He and his family would be forced to live like regular Cubans—and that was if Fidel, that sanctimonious prick, didn't banish him to the Isles of Pines, the Cuban version of Siberia.

He could try to outwit me, figure out where the extra photos were kept and have me arrested. But if he failed, everything would be finished. Better to try to placate me and get me out of his life. I watched all these calculations play out in his expression.

"I want several things. First, you keep bragging about how you have contacts with the American consulate and how you can get visas whenever you want. Well, I need two—one for me and one for a photographer named Luis Rodriguez."

Miguel's eyes flashed, but he kept listening.

I reached into my shirt pocket and pulled out a piece of paper. "All of Luis's information is here."

"Is he your lover?" Miguel spat out the words.

"No. Just another Cuban who wants freedom." I informed him.

Miguel took the paper. "Then I can do it. The hell with you both."

"I also need the necessary documents to bring Pirouette with me." I nodded at the dog, who was watching everything. "And that's the end of it."

"I can do that as well." Miguel seemed relieved that I hadn't asked for anything more. "But you have to leave everything behind that I have given you." I stared at him without saying anything. "You know what that means," he continued. "You can't take the jewelry I gave you. It stays behind, you ungrateful bitch."

The next moments, I knew, were the key to everything. I stood up, walked towards Pirouette's closet, brought out the box where I kept the jewelry that he had given me, and quickly opened it. He caught a glimpse of shining metal and jewelry settings. Then I quickly shut it so he could not closely examine the contents and placed it in a dresser drawer.

"There's a Pan Am flight leaving at one o'clock tomorrow afternoon. I've purchased tickets for Luis and myself. That gives you until morning to get our visas and Pirouette's papers ready."

I went over to another closet and pulled out a small bag. I opened it for him to see the contents. "This is all I'm taking. The jewelry bag and everything else stays here in the apartment." I showed him the several pairs of *pointe* shoes, a photo album with pictures of my family, and a few items of clothing that were inside. He looked at everything sadly.

83

"Leaving with the shirt on your back." He shook his head sadly. "It means that much to you."

"It does." I stared at him, not backing down.

Miguel slowly stood. "You win, Mariana. "You'll get what you want. I'll call you in the morning once I've made the arrangements to let you know when it's done. Just promise me you'll hold up your end. No one sees the pictures."

"If you make sure we get our visas and off the island without any trouble," I warned him. "No one will know your preferences."

He looked at me, and I could see that he was thinking about what had just happened. The jewels were safe in the apartment. If I tried to take the bag full of them, I'd be caught and arrested. He could only hope.

"Just leave with the things you showed me—and your dog—and you'll be fine," he said wearily. "I'll be happy to get rid of that disgusting dog."

"Keep your promise, and no one sees the photos. I give you my word, Miguel."

He nodded, his hands in the pockets of his linen trousers. All the tawdry afternoons had come to this. He had a look of acceptance on his face, probably realizing that he would be done with me in twenty-four hours and that no one would threaten his position in the government or all the benefits he enjoyed. Although he would miss our sexual romps, he suddenly looked glad to be rid of me. And very happy to get rid of Pirouette. I was positive my replacement—for I was positive that I would be quickly replaced—would not be given a dog.

"That's that," he said. He left without another word.

I waited until his footsteps had faded down the hallway before I called for Pirouette.

"Come here, beautiful," I told her. I petted her slowly, turning her collar slowly in my hands, admiring how the beautiful precious stones embedded in its leather caught the light. It was a beautiful, precious sight.

"Wait for me, Rudi," I called out to the moonlit night. "I'm coming to you." I took a deep breath. "I'll be your next Giselle."

Ride Overshare

By Shawn Reilly Simmons

I t wouldn't be so bad, sitting out here all night, if the people who got in the back seat weren't always so dull. Or drunk. I've seen every variety of drunk over the past six months: giggly drunks, angry drunks, soul-searching drunks, amorous drunks, arguing drunks. My policy is to limit pickups to two drunks per ride max, and I stop swiping *Accept* on fares in the bar district after midnight. Drunks tend to tip well, but no amount of money is worth shampooing sour-smelling vomit out of my back seat. One night, a guy broke off his engagement after catching his fiancée swapping spit with his best man outside the bathrooms at the club where I picked him up. They'd been in the kind of place where the music is so loud the windows of my car shake while I wait, idling outside. I wonder how folks can handle noise like that, pounding their heads for hours. When fares come out of those places, they're always yelling, making inane conversation with the back of my head as I haul them home or to the next pulse-pounding club on the strip of bars downtown.

I have my survival kit in my console: bottled water, energy bars, hand sanitizer, masks, and pepper spray. It's not the best idea to pepper spray the interior of a car, but I have it ready in case any nonsense goes down. Luckily, I haven't had to use it yet. Lately, I've thought about slipping a gun in there, too. Not exactly legal, but I've always been an ask for forgiveness not permission kind of person. I started thinking it might be a good idea a few weeks back when a fare decided the top of my face was the prettiest thing he'd ever seen. He gave me the serious creeps. I sped away quickly after it felt like forever for my GPS to find his apartment building. I recognized the look in his eye, the same one I'd been able to dodge in high school on the faces of lust-filled boys and more than one teacher when I wore my cheer squad uniform to class on game days. I learned how to handle the attention then and figured out early that a quick bout of groping after class in the supply closet wasn't a declaration of love. Or even like. High school wasn't that long ago when they told us anything was possible, and a bright future lay ahead. But every year since that time, school feels like an ever-shrinking island I'm drifting away from.

The worst is when I pick up former classmates. The app gives me a first name, and I sometimes decline the fare if I recognize the face in the tiny circle as someone from chemistry class. But I'm not really in a position to turn down cash, so sometimes I have to pull my mask up and slip a cap over my long blonde hair and hope they don't put two and two together. No one makes us wear masks anymore, but they're still a convenient excuse if I'd rather not reveal my entire self to whoever's back there.

I still have dreams; still believe in possibilities. I started the business program at the community college like I'd planned after graduation. But when lockdown came and everything went online, my interest in attending classes went out the window. I did start my cleaning business, though. I only have three clients, but everyone has to start somewhere. It's okay that one of them is my aunt. She's always been way more supportive than my mom, who says vague things like I should be aiming higher, with no explanation or advice on what "higher" might be. She's had the same secretary job for twenty years, the one she got after Dad left and never came back. Growing up, I had to camp out at my aunt's apartment whenever Mom snagged a new boyfriend. Sometimes for a day or two, sometimes a month. The longest time was three months my freshman year. Mom did teach me one important thing: actions speak louder than words. Based on that, I'm pretty sure she shouldn't be handing out advice to anyone regarding life or career choices.

Someday, I'll have a squad of cleaners and direct them to jobs from an office in a building downtown. That's the dream: to be a boss. Signing up for DriveME is just a means to make money to put into my real business. I'm not trying to be a rideshare driver for the rest of my life.

My cleaners will wear lemon yellow uniforms designed to look like cheer uniforms. Every month, each cleaner will book one client for just ten bucks so anyone can have their house cleaned. My company will cover the rest. Having your house cleaned shouldn't just be for rich people. I'm also going to develop a line of non-toxic cleaning products that make washing up cool, targeted to my generation. Like the Skinny Girl Cocktails my mom buys, except for cleaning.

My DriveME app pings, and I look at my tablet. A fare within a mile outside an office building: Jason, 4.5-star rating. It's kind of a weird location because it's already eight at night, and the office parks out that way are usually abandoned at this hour, especially on a Saturday. Maybe he's an entrepreneur like me, working on a project. I tap "accept" and ease away from the curb.

"Late night?" I ask Jason as he slides into the back seat. He's dressed in jeans and a hoodie, not the corporate wear I was expecting, considering the building behind him.

Jason glances at my rearview, a touch of alarm in his eye. "It's only eight."

"Yeah, I meant working late," I say, flicking my eyes at the building.

"Right. Yes," Jason says. He places a green gym bag on the seat next to him and buckles up.

I tap the "heavy" button, indicating I've completed the pickup, and the map swirls on the screen until it zooms in around a pinpoint. The regional airport, forty miles away. The parking lot in the building complex is empty, so I drive across painted rows of parking spaces to the exit. "Taking a trip?" I ask. When I signed up for DriveME, the required fifteen-minute onboarding orientation video encouraged drivers to make polite conversation with "guests" to encourage generous tipping.

A wave of irritation crosses Jason's face. "Yes," he says evenly.

"Somewhere warm, I hope," I say with an encouraging laugh. "These winters start feeling long around February, and all I can do is think about a fruity drink by the ocean."

"What's the ETA?" he asks.

"9:07," I say. "Is that enough time to make your flight?"

Jason eases back against the seat and rubs his eyes, his fingernails short and ragged. "Yeah. They'll wait for me."

A private plane, maybe. I wonder what business Jason is in.

We ride in silence for a few minutes as we make our way through downtown, getting caught at several lights on our way out of the business district. Jason alternates darting glances out the window and rubbing different parts of his face.

"So, what do you do?" I ask at the next red light. I enjoy the conversations with my fares sometimes. It's fascinating what people will tell a stranger just because they're sharing the same few feet of space.

"Crypto," Jason says. "Trading."

"I have no idea how that works. It sounds like Monopoly money to me." I laugh. "Aren't all of those guys in jail now?"

"Not all of them," Jason says, then rubs the stubble on his chin. He isn't the most handsome guy I've ever seen, but there's something about his mouth that's inviting, and the way his eyebrows scrunch together when he is thinking. He's on the hefty side but carries it well. He doesn't seem to be worried about how he looks, which I find appealing, like he has an innate confidence everyone else should pick up on. Jason seems very different from Steve, my high school boyfriend senior year, who looked in the mirror more often than all of the cheer squad put together. Steve got accepted at Louisiana State and broke up with me the next day.

"So, how do you, like, get your money when it's all on the computer?"

Jason laughed sharply, then smiled, the first time since he got in the back seat. "They print it out for you. Banks have special crypto money printers back in their vaults."

It was my turn to laugh. "That sounds made up."

"Sorry, it is," Jason says. "No, it's…crypto is more like digital tokens you can use to pay other people online for things. If that makes sense."

"So why not just use money?" I ask. "Is it like buying stocks or something? I also don't know how the stock market works."

"It's kind of a mix of both," Jason says. "Investors buy units of cryptocurrency and then exchange them like stocks."

"So, how much is a crypto dollar worth?" I ask.

"It's worth as much as someone is willing to pay for it," Jason says. "Hey, would you mind making a stop on the way? The next time you see a mailbox. I need to drop something before I leave."

"Sure," I say. "There's one of the corner of High and Market Streets." I slide to a stop at the next light, making sure to keep the ride smooth for my guest. As I wait for the light to change, I laugh under my breath.

"Something funny?" Jason asks, not unkindly. He seems to have loosened up quite a bit since he first got in the car. Maybe it's my new lavender air freshener. Lavender is a calming herb.

"It's just a little funny…a guy who works with online fake money using an old-school mailbox. Do you want to pick up a newspaper too?" I tease.

"Good one," Jason says, relaxing against the seat. "There are still a few throw-back items that serve a purpose. Postmarks are one. They are tangible proof someone was where they say they were."

"Because timestamps on emails can be faked, right?" I say, making sure not to say much more and reveal how little I know about such things.

"Exactly," Jason says.

"So, what's the name of your crypto thingy?" I ask. "Maybe I should buy some of it as an investment."

Jason's mood darkens as we stop at the intersection of High and Market. He leans forward and lowers his voice. "ShadowCoin," he says. "Don't put your money there." I crane my neck to look as he zips open his duffel bag and pulls out a large envelope with a row of stamps on the front. The words Exchange Commission with a Washington, D.C. address flash before he's out the door and mailing the envelope. I hope he's put enough stamps on it.

"Where did you say you were headed?" I ask when Jason gets back in the car. A light drizzle has started, and I flip on my wipers to clear the glass.

"I didn't," Jason says tersely, then looks into my eyes in the rearview and sighs. "Fortune, Missouri. A cabin in the Ozarks in a tiny town off the map."

"Fortune?" I ask. "What's there?"

"A quiet place for me to…think…until I can figure out what's going to happen next. A college buddy's parents have a cabin on the lake. I haven't talked to him in a while, but I remember where the key is, and they shouldn't be there this time of year."

A worm of worry begins working its way through my stomach. "What if they are there? What will you do then?"

"I'll figure something out," Jason says.

"Is something bad going to happen?" I ask, watching him in the mirror.

Jason locks eyes with mine and says nothing. A tap on a horn behind reminds me the light has turned green.

We continue through downtown, heading for the highway.

"I also have a cleaning business," I say, filling the silence. "I'm just getting started, but I've already had a client accuse me of stealing a necklace from her bedroom, which is insane. Why would I steal from a client I hope to book on a regular basis? After five cleanings, I can buy my own necklace. Of course, she found it the next day in a dresser drawer. All apologies on the phone to me. But the fact she accused me…I just told her I got another gig and let her go." I eye Jason in the rearview. He's staring out the window, and I'm not sure if he's listening to my invented story. "The point is, people make mistakes and do dumb things sometimes."

Jason's eyes meet mine in the mirror, then he shouts, "Red light!"

I slam on the brakes, but it's too late; I'm already halfway through the intersection and have to keep going. The rain has started to come down harder, and it's difficult to see, but that's no excuse. I've broken DriveME's number one rule: keep your eyes on the road, not on the guest.

"Sorry!" I say, my heart pounding. Luckily, no one had started through the intersection yet, but I'd made a dangerous mistake. I resolved to focus for the rest of the ride.

"Look," Jason says. "I don't mean to…you seem like a nice person. I've got to get out of town before—"

Red and blue lights light up the rear window, and Jason and I curse in unison. Loudly. I put on my turn signal and ease to the curb when I see an open spot.

"Don't say anything about anything," Jason says as we anxiously await the officer to walk to the driver's side window.

"I don't know anything. What am I going to say?" I keep my eyes on the mirror. The patrol car door opens, and I squeeze the steering wheel. A moving violation could mean points on my license and an increased insurance premium. Not great for my bottom line.

"You know more than you think you do," Jason says.

A tap on the glass next to my head makes me jump. Rain pings the windshield in fat drops. The police officer has a plastic cover over his wide-brimmed hat that keeps the rain out of his face.

"Good evening, ma'am," he says after I roll down the window. "Did you notice the light back there?"

"Yes, sir," I say, my voice shaking slightly. I'm sorry…I didn't see it. That's no excuse. I apologize."

"It's my fault," Jason says from the back seat.

The officer bends down to get a better look. "What do you mean?"

"I thought she'd made a wrong turn, and I distracted her by trying to get her to double-check the navigation system. I should have trusted my driver to know what she was doing."

"It's the driver's responsibility to follow the rules of the road," the officer says, glancing back at me. "License and registration, please."

"Of course," I say, my heart sinking. I open my console, which does not yet contain a loaded weapon, and hand the items to him.

"Hang tight, I'll be right back," he says, heading back to his patrol car.

"Shit," Jason says once my window is back up.

"Are you in some kind of trouble?" I ask. "Are the cops, like, looking for you?"

"It's…it's complicated," Jason says. "A long story."

"That sounds like a yes. And I've got time."

"It's not like there's an APB out on me. Yet. I still have time to figure things out, I think," Jason said. "I can write new code and change things back to where they were in the beginning. It's just the money part that's going to be a challenge."

The officer steps back into the rain and heads toward us.

"Should I tell him I've got a criminal in my backseat and bargain my way out of this ticket? Maybe get a reward?" I whisper.

"Don't—"

The knuckles on the glass again cut him off. I roll down the window and smile at the officer, hoping a last-ditch charm offensive might save me the fine.

"Please be careful from now on, Miss Finley, especially in inclement weather like tonight. Be safe." He bends down again and speaks to Jason. "And you back there, try not to be so disruptive. This young lady's job is hard enough as it is."

"Yes, sir," Jason says.

As etiquette dictates, I wait for the officer to pull away before easing back onto the road. My heart settles back into a normal rhythm, and I take a few cleansing breaths.

"What are you running from?" I ask him. "And how do you plan to fix things?"

"Teagan Finley," Jason says.

I set my lips in a firm line, keeping my eyes on the road and not on him. "That's right. What? Are you going to try and scare me because you can find out where I live or mess things up for me online? I'm not afraid of you, Jason."

Jason snorted another laugh, which lessened the tension in my shoulders. "No. I've just been wondering what your full name was."

"So now you know. So what?"

"Nothing," Jason says. "When we stopped back there, I mailed everything they'll need to know to investigate ShadowCoin, the company I helped to build from the ground up, the business I've put the last two years of my life into."

"Why?" I asked. "What's going on?"

"The blockchain isn't real. ShadowCoin doesn't have a functional, decentralized ledger recording transactions. It uses a mock-up of a real blockchain to appear legitimate."

"Oh my god, English, please," I say, focusing on the road.

"It's fake," Jason said. "It's made up. Not real. I wrote the code for it. Very soon, thousands of people are going to find out their shares aren't worth anything at all."

"And the real money attached to these shares?" I ask, knowing the answer already.

"Gone," Jason says. "My partners Ponzied it away. Millions."

"Whoa," I say, taking the onramp to the highway. The airport was ten miles away, so we'd be there shortly. "What about you? How much did you manage to squeeze from your unwitting investors?"

"I didn't know what my partners were up to, honestly," Jason says. "I started ShadowCoin with two friends from college. They brought me on to write the code. I wasn't on the sales side. Everything I did was legit. I'm not a thief."

"But you're a partner," I say. "You didn't have any idea?"

"Well," Jason hedges. "Maybe I should have known the numbers looked a bit…inflated. I saw we were doing well and didn't question it as much as I should have. I should have looked harder, been more careful, trusted less. It's no excuse, but my plate is full at work, always putting out fires, patching flaws."

"It's funny," I say, "when people say it's no excuse and then give a list of excuses. Why do we do that?"

Jason laughs and shakes his head. "One day, I answered a call and got an earful from one of our earliest investors. Late payments, unable to access funds. Then I started digging."

"Are you really going to Fortune, Missouri?" I ask.

"To start, and then who knows," Jason says. "I have two years of tuition I didn't use when I dropped out of college to start ShadowCoin. That should carry me for a while. I started stashing that as cash in different places years ago in case—"

"In case you decided to defraud your investors?" I ask, pressing the brake as we head into a curve.

"In case of anything," Jason says. "My partners, let's just say they're not tech-savvy. And they won't be too pleased when they find out I'm gone."

"And all the money you scammed from crypto clients?" I say.

"There's nothing left, as far as I know," Jason says and chews his bottom lip. "As of this evening, my account is worthless."

"What's in the bag?" I asked.

"Evidence," Jason says. "Security."

I look for signs for the private and charter plane fields. "Why don't you turn yourself in and offer to testify against them?" I ask, watching him in the mirror. "Why go on the run at all?"

His face twists between indecision and grief. "My name is on every document, P&L, shareholder agreement, you name it. My lack of action over the last two years is hard to explain. I could spend the rest of my life in jail, even if I do make a deal. I'm twenty-four, and this could make me a felon for life. Because I trusted the wrong people."

I take the next exit and slow down. A scattering of small planes and a hangar building sit off in the distance, barely visible through the rain. The tablet pings, letting me know we've reached our destination.

"It might be good to get some perspective, away from everything for a while," I say.

Jason gathers his things, zips his bag closed, and double-checks the space around him, leaning over to feel under the front seats.

"But then you might want to come back and make things right," I add as he pulls his hoodie over his hair and hitches his bag over his shoulder.

"Be careful out here," Jason says, his hand on the door handle. "And thanks for the ride."

I watch Jason dart through the rain toward the hangar, the wipers swishing water from the glass. I idle near the runway, watching the rain for a few minutes. I could call it a night and head home, get to bed early. I have a house to clean in the morning, a family with four kids. Lots of sticky handprints to scrub away. After several more minutes of staring at the hangar, I slip the car into drive and pull a U-turn.

Something shifts under my seat. I stop the car and reach under, my fingers brushing but not quite reaching something Jason must have left behind. I get out and pull the back door open, reaching under the driver's seat.

A stack of bills with a note tucked under a rubber band appears in my hand. *Fortune favors the bold. Thank you* is scrawled on the note. I get back in the car, my hair soaked with rain, and watch as a small plane taxis down the runway.

The Cemetery Caper: A Childhood Memory

By Verena Rose

Dramatis Personae

- **Jeremy Dimmick:** an out of work father of two who had a plan. It went awry.
- **Evie Ridenour:** your typical twelve-year-old. She loves reading, especially about history. She dreams of becoming an archaeologist.
- **Katie Gast:** Evie's best friend. She's a girly girl who loves clothes.
- **Sgt. Joseph Ridenour:** Evie's father, a cop with a heart.
- **Father Paul:** the Catholic priest who worked a Christmas miracle.
- **Mrs. Ridenour:** Evie's Mom. She's mostly off-stage baking and cooking for Christmas.
- **Mrs. Gast:** Katie's Mom. She always makes sure Evie gets home safely.
- **Mr. Thomas:** the Five and Dime Store Manager. In the end, he got the Christmas spirit.

December 22, 1962 - It's a Saturday

Evie Ridenour is a typical twelve-year-old. She loves helping her mother bake and she passionately loves to read. Today is the first day of Christmas vacation and after helping bake a batch of chocolate chip cookies (her family uses black walnuts), she is heading off to visit her best friend, Katie Gast. Katie only lives one street over, so even though it is still snowing it's an easy walk.

The same day

Standing in front of the local five-and-dime, Jeremy Dimmick isn't sure he can go through with his plan. Recently laid off from his job at the investment firm where he'd worked for more than ten years, he's struggling to provide for his family. So far, he hasn't been able to find another job due to the recent drastic drop in the stock market that was the cause of his company going belly up.

Not able to let his children go without a little something for Christmas, he turns the handle and enters the store. He has worn his big overcoat just for the occasion. And the store is so crowded with last-minute shoppers, he is sure no one will notice if he grabs a couple of small items.

After finding something for each of his two children, he heads for the door, positive he hasn't been seen.

"Stop there!" Mr. Thomas, the store manager, says as he catches hold of Jeremy's arm.

Flustered, Jeremy cringes. "W-What is it?" asks Jeremy, almost stuttering in sudden realization of what he is doing.

"Sir, I think you have some items in your pockets that you've neglected to purchase?"

Lowering his head and audibly sighing, Jeremy turns to face the music. Retrieving the two toys from his coat, he lays them on the checkout counter.

Now very angry, Mr. Thomas says, "I knew you were trying to steal. I'm calling the police. I'm tired of bums like you robbing me blind."

Jeremy is mortified as well as scared. "Sir, I'm so sorry. I lost my job and haven't yet found another. I just wanted to have a little something for my kids on Christmas morning. Would you just let me leave? I promise I'll never enter your store again."

"No, I'm not letting you go! I've lost more merchandise this holiday season than ever before, and I'm going to make an example out of you."

Soon, two patrolmen arrive. After taking the store manager's statement, they handcuff Jeremy and take him off to the jail for processing.

In despair, Jeremy is thinking to himself that now instead of a little something for Christmas he will be spending the holiday in jail.

* * *

That night...

Evie and Katie are having such fun talking about *boys* and what they want for Christmas that they have lost track of time.

Coming to the door of Katie's room, Mrs. Gast says, "Evie, your Mom just called, and she'd like you to come home now. You two get bundled up, and Katie and I will walk you to the gate."

"Okay, Mrs. Gast."

* * *

As she always does after visiting her best friend, Evie takes the shortcut through the Catholic Cemetery. Katie and her mother always walk her to the entrance gate on their street and watch her until the path curves, and they can't see her anymore. There will only be a short time when no one can see her because, once she reaches the gate on the other side of the cemetery, her own street, she knows her mother will be standing at the door watching for her.

On this particular evening, it's bone-chilling cold, and earlier that day, it had snowed. Bundled up in her winter coat, hat, gloves, and snow boots, Evie enters the cemetery. Just to her right and left are the oldest burials in the cemetery. She thinks they might even be the oldest in the entire town. She loves looking at the names of those who lived so long ago—many in the mid to late 1700s. But on this night, the cold is so sharp she knows she shouldn't dawdle.

Unnoticed by Evie, the path between the oldest grave makers is trodden down, but the rest of the path to the far gate is still pristine. She looks around once to make sure Katie and her mother are still there watching her. She raises her arm, waves goodbye, and then continues toward home.

Evie loves this cemetery. Instead of visions of sugarplums, she has visions of someday finding a yet undiscovered Pharaoh's tomb.

Yesterday, in social studies class, her teacher talked to them about the various ways people are buried. She told the students that, in Ancient Egypt, the Pharaohs were buried in huge pyramids, but later, the Egyptians started burying them in a place called the Valley of the Kings, hoping to make it harder for the graverobbers to find. The teacher also explained that, in ancient Rome, they buried their dead outside the city gates and built huge monuments in their memory. Evie is fascinated as she walks by the tombstones and a few of the large vaults in *her* cemetery and wonders who these people were and what they were like.

Suddenly, a sound interrupts her reverie. Evie thinks she hears something.

She stops to listen. Nothing. She takes two more steps and stops. Again, nothing. But she is sure there *had* been something…

She looks around but doesn't see anyone or anything.

Evie, you're being silly. There's no one there. She takes a few more steps, but there it is again. She's still hearing the sounds, like someone crunching on the snow behind her.

In a panic, she starts to run.

Not slowing down, she reaches the far gate, praying that whatever is following doesn't catch her before she can finally get to her mother. Almost falling, she runs through the gate.

Her mother is there, waiting! She keeps running, and even though she knows she'll get reprimanded, she races across the street without looking. She bounds up the steps into the warm safety of home and her mother's arms.

Mrs. Ridenour takes one look at Evie's scared face and knows something is wrong.

"What's gotten into you, Evie? You look like a ghost was chasing you."

"Mom, I couldn't see anything, but I swear I heard footsteps behind me. Maybe it *was* a ghost."

"Dear, were you daydreaming again? I think you were just imagining it. The snow melted a little today, and now it's refrozen. I bet what you were hearing was the sound of your own footsteps crunching the snow."

"Aw, Mom," Evie says as she runs up the stairs to put her coat and snow things into her room.

* * *

December 23, 1962 – the Sunday before Christmas

At breakfast, Evie's father, a city police officer who had worked the night shift, is telling them about a prisoner who had escaped from the jail. Since it is only a few days before Christmas, Sergeant Ridenour isn't looking forward to mounting a manhunt. That could mean some of his squad would not be able to take Christmas Day off to be with their families.

"Dad, what did this prisoner do to be in jail?"

"He stole some small things from Mr. Thomas's store. I'd guess he stole them to give to his children for Christmas. What he took wasn't worth a lot of money, maybe five or ten dollars, but Mr. Thomas caught him and insisted he be arrested."

Evie thinks about that for a minute and says, "That seems awfully harsh considering it's Christmastime."

"I agree. I even offered to pay for the items, but as store manager, Mr. Thomas wanted to make an example of the man. Apparently, he's had a lot of merchandise stolen this shopping season."

Evie, who always loves to hear her father talk about his cases, asks, "How did he escape?"

"After the officers who arrested him finished his processing, they put him in an empty cell and were about to lock it when there was a commotion at the front desk. Apparently, they just pushed the cell door, thinking it was going to lock, but they didn't check it, and the door wasn't completely closed. Because it was the holidays, there was only one man on night duty at the jail, and at some point, he fell asleep. So the prisoner was able to quietly slip out the back door."

"That's so sad. Where do you think he is?"

"I don't know, honey. He hasn't shown up at his house, and he can't go to his mother's because she died around Thanksgiving."

Evie sits in silence, thinking about how lucky her family is, to have a home, for her dad to have a job.

Suddenly, she sits up. "Oh, Dad, I almost forgot! Last night, when I was walking home through the cemetery, I thought I heard footsteps, but I didn't see anyone. I thought it might be a ghost, but Mom told me it was probably my footsteps crunching the ice on top of the snow."

Sergeant Ridenour exchanges glances with his wife but says nothing. But he is thinking, wondering.

* * *

Later, while on duty

That night, Evie's Dad, Sergeant Ridenour, is on duty and in his office at headquarters when he starts thinking again about the story his daughter told him that morning. He is almost sure his wife was correct that Evie's footsteps were crunching the ice on the snow and the sound and echo of that was what she heard. Almost sure. But not positively sure.

Better to investigate the locus, he decides. Putting on his winter gear, he heads out to his cruiser. He drives through town and parks close to the side entrance to the cemetery. He retrieved a high-powered flashlight from his cruiser's trunk and entered the cemetery. He can clearly see his daughter's footprints leading out to the main gate. When he turns on the flashlight, however, its powerful beam reveals another set of footprints veering off to the right. It had been dark out when Evie walked through the cemetery, so she wouldn't have seen them without a flashlight. He notes that the footprints going deeper into the cemetery are large enough to be those of a grown man.

Turning off his flashlight, Sergeant Ridenour starts walking in the same direction as these footprints, trying to be as quiet as possible. After several minutes, the prints stop at a headstone. He can tell that it's a new burial, and he turns on his flashlight to see the name on the stone.

ANN MOORE DIMMICK
Beloved Daughter, Sister, Wife, Mother, and Grandmother
May 14, 1892 – November 20, 1962

As he raises his flashlight, he sees a fresh, obviously homemade Christmas wreath attached to the top of the headstone. He knows now what Evie heard the night before and starts panning the flashlight beam further into the cemetery.

Calling out, he says, "Jeremy, are you in here? Jeremy Dimmick, this is Sergeant Ridenour of the City Police. If you're in here, please come out. You need to go back to the jail. This isn't helping your family."

Moving as carefully and quietly as he can, Ridenour begins walking along the line of gravestones, searching for more footprints. As he turns to go back along the row, he notices what at first looks like a pile of rags. He bends down to investigate and realizes it's Jeremy Dimmick, his escaped prisoner.

"Jeremy, wake up. It's me, Sergeant Ridenour. I need to get you back to the jail."

Jeremy doesn't respond. Ridenour tries again to wake the man with no success. He then checks to see if there is a pulse. Thankfully, there is. He knows he'll have to get this man to the hospital as soon as possible. He retraces his steps back to the side gate and leaves the cemetery.

He hasn't realized how cold he is until he slides back into his cruiser. Turning on the ignition to get some heat going, he keys up his microphone and calls headquarters.

"Dispatch, this is Sergeant Ridenour. I need you to call an ambulance to the St. John Catholic Cemetery right away. Over."

"10-4 Sarge. Are you hurt?" asks the dispatcher.

"No, I've found Jeremy Dimmick lying next to his mother's grave. He's alive but not conscious. Tell the ambulance to enter by the side gate and no sirens. Over."

"Roger that, Sarge."

Opening the cruiser's trunk, Ridenour takes out the emergency blanket from the first aid kit. He hurries back to the unconscious man and does his best to cover him up. Knowing he shouldn't move an unconscious man without knowing if and how he might be injured, this is all he feels able to do. Feeling helpless now, he heads back to his cruiser to wait for the ambulance.

About ten minutes later he sees the ambulance arrive, so he gets out of his very warm cruiser to lead the ambulance attendants to Jeremy.

"Come on, let's get him out of the cold as soon as we can. I'm sure he'll need medical attention once you get him to the hospital."

"Isn't he your escaped prisoner? Are you going to handcuff him?" asks one of the ambulance attendants.

"Yes, he is, but under the circumstances, handcuffs aren't necessary. He's not going anywhere tonight, and I'll assign an officer to stay outside his room once he's been admitted.

* * *

December 24, 1962 – Christmas Eve

The next evening, while Sergeant Ridenour is home on his dinner break, he is working the crossword puzzle in that day's paper, as he always does. When Evie comes bounding into the room, full of energy, he decides it's time to tell her about finding his escaped prisoner.

"Hey, Evie girl, come over and sit with your Dad for a few minutes. I'll be leaving soon to go back on patrol, and I wanted to tell you what happened last night."

"What's up, Dad?"

"You remember you told me about coming through the cemetery the other night and that you thought you heard footsteps?"

"Yes, I remember. But you and Mom convinced me that it was just the ice crunching."

"Well, that next evening, when I was sitting in my office, I started thinking about your story. You see, I remembered that our escaped prisoner was Catholic, and I also remembered that his mother had recently passed away."

"Really, Dad? So you were thinking maybe you could pick up his trail in the cemetery?"

"That's right, Evie, I did."

"Come on, Dad, don't keep me in suspense. Did you find him?"

"Yes, and not a moment too soon. I found him curled up behind his mother's headstone, unconscious. I called for an ambulance to be dispatched and had him taken to the hospital."

"Oh, that poor man. Do you think you can convince the five-and-dime store manager to drop the charges so he can be home with his family for Christmas tomorrow?"

"I don't know. But I'm going to go visit Father Paul this evening to see if he will put in a good word for Jeremy. After all, he wouldn't be the first man in his profession to stand up for a good thief!"

* * *

.

Later that evening at the Catholic Church

Hoping his idea will work, Sergeant Ridenour parks his cruiser and makes his way to the door of the church rectory. Pressing the doorbell, he waits for the door to be opened.

"My goodness, son, what are you doing out on a night like this? Get yourself in here so you can warm up." Father Paul is well known and much loved in the neighborhood for the work he does for the community, especially for the homeless and others in need.

"Thank you, Father Paul. I'm still on duty, and I'm hoping you can help me with something."

Offering the Sergeant a chair in the rectory's parlor, Father Paul says, "Of course, I'll help if I can."

"I don't know if you heard about our escaped prisoner or not, but he's one of your congregants, so I thought you'd be the best person to ask for help. His name is Jeremy Dimmick. He recently lost his job and is still unemployed. Feeling he was out of options, he attempted to steal toys for his children from the five-and-dime. The manager of the store caught him during his feeble attempt at petty larceny and insisted on pressing charges."

"Joseph, yes, I know the Dimmicks very well. They are regular attendees at Sunday Mass, but now that I think on it, I don't remember seeing them yesterday. Poor Virginia, she and the children must be devastated. And just so you know, Gary Thomas, the manager of that store, is also one of my flock. What would you like me to do?"

"First, would you mind calling the store? I just passed there, and they are still open, attending to last-minute shoppers. Maybe you can convince Mr. Thomas to drop the charges. I would love to be able to send Jeremy home tonight."

"I will call right away. And if needed, I'll go see Gary in person."

"Thank you, Father Paul. Please call me at the station and let me know what happens."

"And God bless you, Joseph, for caring."

When Sergeant Ridenour gets home very late, well, very early on what is now Christmas morning, the house is quiet. Evie and her mother have both gone to bed, having spent the day baking cookies, preparing the turkey and all of the other delicious things for their holiday dinner.

Joseph Ridenour smiles to himself as he fills the stockings on the mantel. This is going to be a very special Christmas with a very special surprise.

* * *

December 25, 1962 – Christmas Day

On Christmas morning, Evie is bursting with excitement, eager to open her presents. She's been so busy the last few days before Christmas, she's forgotten all about her scare in the cemetery and she's forgotten all about Jeremy Dimmick.

As anxious as she is to get the presents, the rule in her family is you have to eat breakfast first. Otherwise, her parents know food will be forgotten in the wake of opening packages.

At the breakfast table, her dad looks at her and says, "Evie, aren't you going to ask me about Mr. Dimmick?"

"Who?" Evie asks.

"You've forgotten already? I guess the excitement of Christmas overshadowed everything else. Remember: Jeremy Dimmick, the escaped prisoner?"

"Oh. Sorry, Dad, I did sort of forget. What happened to him?"

"Fortunately, this story has a very happy ending. Last night, Father Paul called and spoke with the store manager, and it was agreed that he would drop the charges as long as Jeremy was given a warning. Knowing the dire circumstances Jeremy and his family were experiencing, Father Paul was also able to arrange gifts for the children as well as a Christmas dinner with all of the fixings."

"Oh, wonderful, Dad. What an extra special Christmas this is!"

"It is, indeed," Mrs. Ridenour says, smiling at the husband she knows had had a lot to do with the happy ending for the Dimmick family.

Christmas afternoon

Evie's friend Katie has come visiting. Up in Evie's room, as twelve-year-old girls will do, they are comparing their gifts and making plans for the rest of their time off from school.

"Katie, I have the most marvelous news. You remember the night I thought someone was following me in the cemetery? There really was someone in the cemetery. My dad checked into it, and that's where he found his missing prisoner."

"Wow, Evie, your Dad's a hero."

"Yes, and I helped him solve the case. He told me things could have been far worse if I hadn't told him about my walk through the cemetery that night. The man he was looking for had almost frozen to death. His name is Jeremy Dimmick. The reason he was trying to steal was for his children, but his plan was a disaster."

"Maybe when you grow up, you'll be on the police force like your Dad."

"No, not me. While I do like mysteries and solving things, I really want to be an archaeologist or an historian and study about people who lived in the past."

Katie laughs at her friend and says, *"Boring!"*

* * *

December 26, 2023

Years later, when Evie is all grown up, old even, she hasn't realized her dream of being an archaeologist, but she has indeed realized her dream of becoming an historian. She often wonders whether the time spent walking through St. John Cemetery was the beginning of it all. Especially her love of cemeteries.

It has been many years since she's visited that cemetery. Snow is on the ground, just as it was then, and she knows she'll have to walk through some crunchy ice. But off she goes. She parks her car near the side wrought-iron gate and enters as she always had as a girl. There they are, still standing, those ageless gravestones from long ago. She now knows that these graves belong to some very interesting people, including French settlers who fled the St. Dominique Slave revolt of 1791. One family, that of Etienne Bellumeau de la Vincendiere, made their way here from Charleston, South Carolina.

She decides to take a walk further into the cemetery, finally arriving at the burial site she is looking for: Ann Moore Dimmick. And next to it there is now another headstone, this one for Ann's son, Jeremy Dimmick. The desperate father from so long ago. Evie offers up a silent prayer for the man her father had saved from freezing. She hopes he had had a good life.

She remains by his graveside thinking about all of the wonderful and interesting places she had visited during her career researching burial traditions both in America and abroad.

Upon reflection, she thinks the favorite cemeteries she had visited are St. Louis No. 1 in New Orleans, Louisiana; Hollywood Cemetery in Richmond, Virginia; and the *Pere Lachaise* Cemetery in Paris, France.

Maybe New Orleans is her favorite. In addition to St. Louis No. 1, she had also visited Lafayette Cemetery. On the day she stood in front of Madame Marie Leveau's tomb, she had imagined hearing the distant drums from Congo Square. Her greatest regret is never getting to Egypt. She so wants to visit the tomb of Tutankhamun. Well, she isn't dead yet!

She remembers the day she heard footsteps in the snow in St. John Cemetery. Yes. That was the day her imagination and thirst for knowledge became one. Ironic how Mr. Dimmick's failed Christmas caper helped merge these two qualities into an exciting and worthwhile career. Had it failed?

Sighing, Evie lays her hand on Jeremy Dimmick's headstone. "Rest in peace, Jeremy."

With a smile, already thinking about more adventures in her future, she turns and leaves the quiet solitude of St. John Cemetery.

Sutton's Law

By John Shepphird

My neighbor Keith was a thief. And I became his apprentice.

I was enrolled at El Camino Community College. It was supposed to be the path to get into a legit university to earn a four-year degree. At least, that's what my high school counselor told me. But I only enrolled to get my parents off my back. School was a bore. My apartment was near campus, wedged up against L.A.'s 405 Freeway. The traffic noise bothered me at first, especially with the window open. After a while I got used to it—a hum of white noise to help me drift off to sleep.

Keith moved in next door, and I saw him coming and going. He was a few years older than me, had long hair tied back. He wore a Las Vegas Raiders cap and sometimes a faded BYU sweatshirt. He said he came from Salt Lake City. Because of the BYU sweatshirt, I asked if he was Mormon. "Jack Mormon," he said.

"What's that?"

"I was raised Latter Day Saint, but now prefer to drink, smoke, and tell lies," Keith said with a cackle-laugh to reveal broken teeth. He seemed like an alright guy, didn't have any furniture, or even a TV, so I invited him over to watch Thursday Night Football since the Raiders were playing. He said that he came to L.A. to find work in the film and TV industry. We found common ground smoking weed and watching old movies. Heist movies and film noirs were Keith's favorites.

Both of us were broke. Our larceny started by sneaking Tupperware into buffets, small stuff like that. Most of the time, we managed to sneak past the register. When we couldn't, one of us would pay and distract the staff while the other shuttled containers out to my car. Keith had all this random trivia in his head and told me once, "Herb McDonald was the marketing genius that created the first 24-hour all-you-can-eat buffet at the El Rancho Vegas. Only cost a dollar back then, so they named it the Buckaroo Buffet. Soon, every casino had one. The dude could see the future." Keith knew a lot about vintage Vegas stuff. He threw around names like Benny Binion and Wilbur Clark, guys I'd never heard of. He claimed most of the land in Clark County is owned by Mormons.

"Jack Mormons?"

"Nah," he said, "Real ones. Hypocrites. You know why you can't invite just one Mormon fishing? You need to bring two, or he'll drink all your beer."

We lived near LAX so hit hotel breakfast buffets. Nobody checks your room key. Leaving with a paper plate looks like you're heading back to your room. Crashing weddings meant free booze. We got secondhand sports jackets at Goodwill. Just show up and don't talk to anyone. Throw a buck or two in the tip jar and ask for a double, then keep 'em coming. Once a girl even asked me to dance.

About the time Keith became my neighbor I was working part time at a temp agency. One day lifting shelving fixtures at a Ross Dress for Less I tweaked my back. Keith taught me how to collect Worker's Compensation. I wasn't in pain, but free money is free money. He had all the angles.

There was this girl Ruthie in my economics class. I'd been fantasizing about her. She mostly wore heels and short skirts, showing off her awesome legs. Ruthie always came to school dressed up, not like most of the other girls. I figured she went directly from class to a fancy office job or something.

After class one day, outside, she was talking on her phone and her purse strap broke. She didn't notice. I picked it up and caught up with her. "I think this yours," I said, holding the strap to show that it broke.

"Oh my God, thanks," she said and finished her call. "My license and credit cards are in there. Thanks so much. We're in econ class together, right?"

"I'm Mike," I said.

"I know. I'm Ruthie."

"Kind of a thin strap on that purse of yours," I said. "Maybe have that looked at."

Examining it, in a hushed voice, she said, "Oh...Don't tell anyone, but it's a Saint Laurent knock-off. No wonder it broke."

"Knock-off?"

"The real one cost seventeen hundred bucks."

I winked. "Your secret's safe with me."

We made casual conversation—talked about the weird economics professor we shared. Turns out we were both from the South Bay, and our high schools were bitter rivals. She teased me about our lame football team.

"You must have been a cheerleader," I said.

"Why do you say that?"

"I don't know. Cause you're so beautiful."

"Thank you," she said, blushing. "But, no...not me. I hung out with the stoners, mostly," she laughed.

We had that in common.

She thanked me again and moved on. I caught her looking back, so I smiled and waved before heading back to my car. We'd made a connection, for sure. I knew I had to work up the nerve to ask her out—*had* to take that shot.

I was daydreaming, on cloud nine, until I reached my 2005 Honda Accord. That's when I realized there was no way I could pick her up in my car. A girl as classy as Ruthie wouldn't be caught dead in my junkyard heap. It had over two hundred thousand miles, the dash was cracked, and the upholstery torn. The air conditioner didn't work, and there was a weird odor I couldn't track down. I'd taken a girl from high school out in it, and then she ghosted me forever.

There was this BMW I'd seen around I thought looked cool, the two-door coupe 2 Series. And I'd seen a commercial about leasing options, so stopped into the dealership to see what it would cost.

"How's your day going?" the salesman said. He wore all black, his hair slicked back, came off as sort of a douchebag. "I'm Sergio. Let me know if you have any questions."

I said, "I'm thinking about leasing a car," and asked him how that worked.

"If I can borrow my driver's license for a brief credit check," he said, "we can explore the options." We went into the showroom and did just that. But I had no real credit history, nor could I provide proof of employment. But he said there are ways around that. If I put twenty-five hundred dollars down, my monthly payment would be just over nine hundred dollars.

That was impossible. I said, "Yeah, don't think I can afford that."

"What can you afford?"

"Is there a no money down option?"

"Unfortunately, not for the Ultimate Driving Machine." He gave me his card, and that was that.

I figured to take Ruthie out, maybe I could rent a car. But because I was under twenty-five, there'd be a surcharge. You can't win.

The next day, Keith knocked on my door with a backpack slung over his shoulder and said, "Dude, gonna need your help. Got a second?" Before I could reply, he brushed past me, opened my fridge, and dug out a can of Natty Ice for himself. It's what he always did when he came over—drank my beer and nibbled on whatever was in the fridge since we'd stolen most of it together. Budweiser's Natural Ice comes in thirty packs. For the price, it's one of the cheapest beers with the highest kick, like malt liquor, most bang for your buck. Keith said, "You realize I only have my bike, right?" He got around on a Suzuki dirt bike chained to the carport outside. "Well...I'm gonna need a driver."

"For what?"

He cracked open his beer and sipped, toasted me with, "To boost baby formula. Scouted a store full of 'em, and I've got a fence that pays cash."

"Baby formula?"

"Hell yeah."

I said, "What if someone sees my car?"

"Like who?"

"Security cameras."

He pulled a stack of assorted license plates from his backpack. "We'll duct tape one of these over your plate. Your black Honda...there's millions of them on the road."

I was hesitant and told him so.

Keith said, "All I need you to do is wait outside in the car. I'll get the stuff, load it all in, and we're off," he said, motioning with his palm like an airplane taking flight.

"I don't know, dude..."

"What's your problem?"

"What if my car breaks down?"

"Your car isn't going to break down," he said. "You'll keep it running the whole time."

I told him I'd think about it.

He called me "chicken-shit" and danced around, clucking aloud and flapping his elbows. "Grow some balls, why don't ya? All I need is a driver."

"What if we get busted?

"Haven't you read the papers? Nobody gets busted for shoplifting anymore. Even store security guards can't do shit. It's the law. Theft insurance covers the loss for the stores."

I kept refusing, but Keith had a way to wear me down.

That night we taped one of his license plates on my car and drove to the Ralphs supermarket he'd cased. He had me pull up to the curb, and said, "Unlock your doors. Wait here. And be cool." Keith pulled up his hoodie, got out, and slinked inside. I was nervous, could almost hear my heart beating as I looked around to make sure nobody was watching.

A couple of minutes later, he wheeled out two shopping carts, loaded them in the trunk, and then more in the back seat. The overflow went in the passenger seat and my lap. He slammed the door, and we were off. "Like shooting fish in a barrel," he said.

We drove out to Long Beach. In the parking lot of a Denny's he sold the cans to some scary-looking dude with a graffiti-covered cube truck. Five dollars each. Keith gave me half the take. Then, we drove to the dispensary to score weed.

To get into a legal dispensary you need a driver's license as a requirement to make sure you're over twenty-one. Keith said he didn't have one, claimed the "government took it." He wrote down a list of specific brands and pre-rolls he wanted me to show to the clerk.

We'd smoked a bowl, played *Grand Theft Auto* on my Xbox, and finished the coconut shrimp and Kung Pao chicken we'd scored from the Asian buffet the night before.

I told Keith I was thinking about leasing a BMW. I had some money, but not enough for a decent car. Keith talked about his plan to lasso an ATM. "There's one we can snag. Looks easy. Full of cash."

"That's crazy," I said.

"Ever hear of Sutton's Law?"

"No."

"It means look for the complete obvious. Also known as the Willie Sutton Rule."

"What are you talking about?"

"Everyone knows there's money in those things, right? It's just sitting there asking to be taken. That's where the *Law* comes into play."

"The law of averages?"

"No. Aren't you listening? Sutton's Law. Willie Sutton was a bank robber back in the olden days. Badass, but never killed anyone. He was a player, too, always had hot chicks on his arm. Slick Willie hit all these banks, escaped from prisons…then one day a reporter asked him why he robbed banks, and Willie said, 'because that's where the money is.'"

"Like this ATM."

"Correctamundo, my friend. What Willie was saying is look for the *obvious,* where the money is. And now Sutton's Law is a term used by doctors to mean don't overthink it," he pressed his thumb on his nose with, "the diagnosis is as plain as the nose on your face." Keith could talk bullshit, especially after he'd smoked the sativa, but this took the cake. "Sutton's Law, my friend. All I need is a driver."

"How's an ATM gonna fit in my car?"

"We're not taking your car, bro. I've got a pickup. I just need your help driving and lifting it into the bed."

"I don't think that's a good idea."

"Why do you say that?"

"A bank will have *serious ass* security cameras."

"I've got that covered," Keith took a hit from my bong, held it in a dramatic pause, then exhaled with a raspy cough. He sat back and elaborated, "I'll use my paintball gun," his finger pointed like a pistol, "to splotch all the camera lenses first."

"I don't know, dude..."

"We'll split the take fifty-fifty."

"Count me out."

"Bro?" He showed me pictures he'd taken on his phone. It was a drive-up ATM at a bank, not set in the wall of the building but rather on a concrete island at the drive-up. "Here's the cameras," he said, pointing to sections of the photos he'd taken. "I'll take those out, ninja style. We'll wait to see if anyone comes. If no security or cops come around, then we'll pull the ATM out this way," suggesting a direction to drag the machine.

"With what?"

"This truck." He showed me another photo of a pickup parked in the driveway of a suburban home.

"So we're robbing a bank *and* stealing a car?"

"It's not a car, it's a truck."

"What? You gonna hot wire it or something?"

"No." Keith reached into his pocket and produced a key to show me. "I got a copy made of the key."

"How'd you do that?"

"I found the listing on craigslist , been kicking the tires, pretending like I was interested in buying it. Asked the owner if I could take it to my mechanic first for him to take a look under the hood. He was cool with that, but I didn't take it to no mechanic, dude. Instead, I had a key made." Keith seemed proud of his ingenuity.

I said, "I don't think this is a good idea."

"Got a better one?"

"*Not* do it."

"That's not an option, bro."

"So, you pull this ATM off its base and get it into the truck," I said. "Then what?"

"Find a quiet place and take my Sawzall to it. Easy-peasy." Keith's favorite power tool was the Milwaukee Sawzall, a handheld, cordless saw. He confessed he'd used it to steal catalytic converters. "Afterward, we'll return the truck to the guy's driveway, and he's none the wiser."

"I wish I could help you," I said, not meaning it, "but I just can't."

"I thought you were my friend."

"You'll have to find someone else."

"There is nobody else." He was clearly disappointed.

I told him that I had a test tomorrow and needed to study, so he hang-dogged out of my apartment, cursing under his breath. But the walls of the complex were thin, and I could hear him clucking like a chicken next door, clearly intended for me. Occasionally he'd yell out "chicken shit" or "weasel boy," followed by more clucking. That went on most of the night.

The next morning, on my way to class, Keith opened his door and said, "Hey dude, sorry about last night. If you don't want to help, that's totally cool. Just...you've got to keep this on the down low. Don't say anything to anybody."

"Your secret's safe with me." The same thing I'd said to Ruthie about her replica purse.

"Thanks, bro. All good."

I asked, "How much do you think is in that ATM?"

"Anywhere between thirty to fifty thousand. Maybe more."

"Seriously?"

"Gonna hit it the Wednesday before Thanksgiving so it will be loaded up before Black Friday and the four-day weekend." I must admit the idea of twenty-five thousand dollars in cash intrigued me. Keith said, "But I understand if you're scared, bro. I won't judge."

* * *

When she came into class that day, Ruthie gave me a wave. It *was* time to ask her out. What's that proverb? *He who hesitates is lost.*

I sat through the lecture, watching her. I'd never seen her so beautiful, wearing a tight-knit dress that hugged in all the right places. After class, I worked up the courage to walk up and say, "Hey. Did you get that purse fixed?"

"Not yet. What's up, Mike?"

I said, "Same old," trying to sound cool, realizing that was awkward phrasing. I continued, "I was wondering, you want to grab a coffee or something? Before you're off to work."

"Work?"

"I figured you dress up to go to an office after class."

"You think I dress up?" she said accusingly.

"Not really, but more than other girls. I, uh…like your style."

That landed. I could see it in her eyes. Ruthie obviously liked being complimented. "Thank you. No, I don't have a job. Working on it. I guess I could go for a Frappucino."

Bingo.

At the Starbucks near campus, we got to know each other more. She talked about her aspirations to travel and see the world. I listened mostly, but my mind was focused on making love to her, which made me speechless. That worked out okay because she did most of the talking anyway. What became entirely clear was that I had to impress her. I *needed* to advance the ball.

She thanked me for the coffee, and before we parted random talk led us to talking about food. We compared notes on what South Bay restaurant made the best tacos. I had my opinion. She had hers. Spontaneously, I said, "We need to compare, check out both places. Let's do that. When are you free?"

Ruthie said, "I'm real busy with family stuff all through Thanksgiving." That sounded like a rejection. I braced myself, but then she said. "So, how about the weekend after?"

Ruthie was the reason I agreed to lasso the ATM.

* * *

I'd brought latex gloves to not leave fingerprints behind. Technically, it was Thanksgiving Day, after 1:00 a.m. by the time we set out. I followed Keith on his motorcycle to the Culver City neighborhood where the truck was parked. It was sort of like we were playing *Grand Theft Auto,* but now for real.

I parked a couple of blocks away on a side street and he walked for the truck. When he returned in the pickup it was bigger than what I'd imagined from the photo. It had a cattle guard in front with a reinforced tow bar on the back. Keith dropped the tailgate, and we hoisted his motorcycle into the bed. "Getaway insurance," he said, and he strapped it into the truck bed.

I drove the truck as Keith directed me to a pile of wooden pallets behind a dumpster where he'd stashed a roll of chain, a crowbar, a sledgehammer, and assorted padlocks. All the tools were still in their original packaging. I asked, "Where'd you get this stuff?"

"Home Depot," he said, thumbing over his shoulder.

Next, we drove past the bank a few times and circled back to tuck back into the darkened parking lot across the street. From there, we had a view of everything. Keith said, "Wish me luck." With his paintball gun, he ducked out and crossed the street, circumvented the bank, and shot at the corners of the building, followed by more shots up under the carport.

I was nervous and sweating, wanted to take the latex gloves off but knew I couldn't. A light rain began to fall. Keith finished his work and returned. "Now we wait. If nobody shows up, we're in business."

We had time to kill, so we spent it talking about all sorts of things. I told him about Ruthie and how I'd asked her out. With the money, my plan was to lease a car she wouldn't be embarrassed to be seen in.

"Your car is fine, dude," Keith said. "If she doesn't like it, tell her to screw." I realized then that when Keith talked about girls, he always referred to them as "skanks" and "nasty bitches." Not a lot of respect. He said, "I had a cool girlfriend once...but then she turned *uncool.* Bitched all the time. Had to dump her ass."

I asked, "So what are you going to do with the money?"

"It's bad luck to even think about it."

"Maybe you should get some furniture," I suggested.

"Maybe."

Rain obscured the view from the windshield, so every once in a while, I had to engage the wipers. Other than an occasional car driving past, nobody came. After more than an hour, Keith said, "Okay, let's do it."

I drove into the bank parking lot. He got out and directed me under the carport. "I'll hook this bad boy up, then give you the signal. Back up, and I'll connect to the hitch."

"Got it."

I watched from inside the cab as he wrapped the ATM machine with great care, pulling the chain taught before fastening each padlock. He directed me to ease the truck into a spot so the ATM it would clear the concrete barriers on each side. Through the truck's backup camera, I could see Keith secure the chain to the trailer hitch. I had visions of truck commercials with guys wearing flannel pulling out tree stumps. Keith came up to the driver's side. "Okay, move over."

"I'm the driver."

"This is a man's job."

I hopped over the console, and Keith climbed in. He backed the truck up to give the chain some slack before putting it in drive and punching the gas. The Dodge Ram lurched forward but stopped with a jolt. I could hear the tires spin. The pavement was wet, so I'm sure that didn't help.

Keith cursed and put the truck in reverse, slowly backing up to give the chain some more slack. He hit the gas again. Another lurch, and we were stopped once more, back tires spinning. Smoke bellowed behind us. Keith cursed and clenched his teeth, threw the truck in reverse, and stomped the gas.

We sped backwards. The rear end of the pickup smashed into the ATM with a loud crash. Then, he drove forward some, backed up, and rear-ended the machine again. That didn't work. The truck's tires spun on the pavement. It dawned on me, and I said, "Put it in four-wheel drive."

Keith thought about that for a second, snapped his fingers, and tried that strategy. Four-wheel drive worked. The ATM was ripped clean off the concrete perch. We dragged it to the back of the parking lot and came to a stop in the alley. "Load her up," he said. But before either of us could get out, headlights appeared in the alley up ahead. Whoever it was, they were coming our way. Keith panicked. He shifted to drive, punched the gas, and drove straight at them. I turned to see the ATM dragging behind us, bouncing and swinging from side to side.

The headlights ahead slowed and came to a stop, but Keith kept going, like a game of chicken. At the last minute, he cut the wheel and swerved around them. I could see it wasn't cops, or a security guard, just a car full of teenagers with fear in their eyes.

Keith drove on laughing. The ATM was like a ball-and-chain dragging behind, sparking off the wet pavement.

He made a hard right. The ATM rolled and slammed into a parked car. That set off its alarm. Keith cursed, slammed on the brakes. The ATM came forward and crashed into the back of the truck. We both jumped out. Keith tried to open the tailgate, but it had been so damaged from when he rear-ended the machine, it wouldn't budge. When it became obvious the gate would not come down, and with the car alarm sounding down the street, he ordered, "Lift it. Come on."

That's when things got complicated. I should have used my legs, not my back. I felt a jolt of pain as we struggled to lift the machine over the tailgate. It was the back injury from before, my Workman's Compensation claim. Suddenly it was very real, and very painful.

I buckled over, and Keith had to take over. The machine teetered until finally, he was able to push it over the tailgate, and it toppled into the truck bed with a boom. Lights went on in the houses around us. As Keith pulled the chain into the truck bed, I managed to climb back into the passenger seat, wincing in pain.

We hauled ass away. When it was clear we weren't being followed, Keith began to laugh. My back was killing me. I felt like I was going to throw up.

In a vacant lot he found cover behind trees. Keith jumped into the truck bed and managed to kick the tailgate open. With the crowbar, he worked to pry open the ATM. The thing was like a clamshell, next to impossible to open. With the Sawzall, and a few slugs from the sledgehammer, he was able to break off the cover.

Inside was a skeleton of metal struts. I held the flashlight as Keith went to work with the crowbar and hammer. He was soon covered in sweat and out of breath. He handed me the crowbar, and I went to work. The goal was the money tray buried deep inside.

Finally, it was visible, revealing stacks of $100 and $20 bills bound under rubber cams. I pried the rollers away. That's when I heard a pssst sound and felt the spray. I pulled my hand back to see it covered in red ink. The thing was booby-trapped.

Keith jumped in. He peeled bills from the trays and stuffed them in his backpack. I could see some of the money was stained with ink, but not as bad as my hand. That's when I saw the flashing lights in the distance. Cops were coming.

Keith didn't miss a beat. He unstrapped his motorcycle from the truck bed and rolled it out. He hoisted his backpack over his shoulder, climbed on his bike, and kick-started it to life. "Sayonara," he said and sped off across the dirt field. With all the money, my partner in crime disappeared into the night.

The sound of his motorcycle was overtaken by sirens. I ran. With my back in so much pain I didn't get far. The cops tackled me hard. They held guns against my head and cuffed me.

* * *

Had the ATM been sitting in a retail store and not at a bank, the money would not have been insured by the Federal Reserve. Because Keith chose a bank, FBI agents questioned me. I stupidly told them everything before even asking for a lawyer. I explained how Keith was my neighbor, how we'd burglarized Ralphs for baby formula and scammed buffets. As an apprentice thief nobody ever taught me not to say anything, ever, but it was too late, they had my confession.

Giving up Keith didn't really matter because there was nothing to connect him to the crime. I came to learn he wasn't paying rent next door, just living there as a squatter. Somehow, he'd scammed a key. That explained why he had no furniture.

They asked me his last name, but I didn't know it because I'd never asked. They didn't believe me. I'm not even sure if Keith was his real first name. Maybe it was Jack. Jack Mormon who "drank, smoked, and lied."

I learned that ATM bank machines have GPS tracking devices inside. That's how the cops found us so fast. Keith got away with the money, I was caught red handed, literally, with dye pack ink on my hands as evidence to connect me to the crime. This wasn't Sutton's Law. It was criminal law.

Later, I learned some of the stained cash was found in casino slot machines in Vegas. I guess Keith is laundering the money. Doesn't surprise me. I'm sure he's out there scheming somewhere, convincing another neighbor to drive him around.

Nowadays, my buffet is served at the Federal Correctional Institution in Victorville, California. The prison cafeteria is never all-you-can-eat. There's no Tupperware to take any of it back to your cell, not that you'd want to. I don't have a window in my cell and miss the sound of L.A.'s 405 Freeway that I once took for granted. At night, in prison, you fall asleep to slamming doors, crazies screaming, and nocturnal chatter.

From time to time, I think about Ruthie and wonder what she's doing. Time is what I've got. Plenty. Time to regret that I'd become an apprentice thief.

Grandpa Minds the Baby

By Marcia Talley

My daughter stands in the open doorway of her condo next to an over-stuffed wheelie carry-on. A garment bag from Nordstrom is draped over her arm.

"Are you sure?" she asks, looking worried. "It's not too late to change your mind."

I open the door wide, keeping a hand on the knob. "Don't be silly," I tell her. "You've got the dress and the shoes and that feathery thing for your hair." I pause, trying to remember what it's called.

"A fascinator," she supplies.

"Go, go…" I say, making shooing motions with my free hand. "The Uber's waiting. Charlie and I will be just fine. Don't worry."

From the infant seat where he's been so recently smothered with kisses, Charlie agrees. "Blurp," he says.

"I could always take Charlie with me…" she offers for the third time that morning.

For the third time, I cut her off. "To a Las Vegas wedding? Married by an Elvis impersonator crooning 'Love Me Tender'? Not on my watch."

Tansy frowns in mock exasperation. "It's not *that* kind of wedding, Dad. It's a class act. On the terrace by the fountains at the Bellagio."

"No Elvis? How can the marriage even be legal?" I lean forward and kiss her cheek. "You'll be the prettiest bridesmaid at the ceremony, wherever they decide to hold it."

"The only thing missing is Peter," she says, hooking the strap of her handbag securely over her shoulder.

"It's only a week," I remind her. "Charlie and I will be fine, won't we Charlie? We'll hang out with the guys at the Strike Zone, bowl a few games, chow down at MickeyD's..."

She leans in, gives my cheek a peck. "No funny business now, boys. Not like the last time."

I once took my grandson to a NASCAR race in Richmond, and a car spun out into the stands. Tansy's memory is long. "No worries," I promise. I grasp my daughter firmly by the shoulder and escort her into the eighteenth-floor vestibule of the high-rise apartment she shares with my son-in-law. Peter's deployed to the Persian Gulf with the USS Eisenhower carrier strike group. Indefinitely. She waggles her fingers at her baby boy, blows him a kiss. "Be good for Grandpa," she coos, "and Mama will bring you a surprise from Las Vegas."

"Bye-bye, bye-bye," Charlie says.

I watch from the window until my daughter's Uber exits the horseshoe in front of Lighthouse Towers and heads north along Shore Drive toward the Norfolk Airport. Then I fix Charlie a bottle of milk, pop the top on a can of Bud Light, and settle onto the sofa with my grandson. I reach for the remote and aim. "Let's see how the Ravens are doing, buddy."

We tune into the game, swigging happily. I cringe when Lamar Jackson fumbles and Steelers linebacker T.J. Watt picks up the loose ball.

Charlie belches, equally unimpressed.

Charlie and I are wrapping up dinner—microwave mac and cheese for me and spaghetti hoops for Charlie—when Tansy FaceTimes from the Bellagio, reporting in. "All's good here," I tell her, "but the Ravens blew an early lead and lost to the Steelers 17 to 10."

"Pity," she says flatly. Tansy says that watching football is like being stuck in heavy traffic—stop and start, stop and start. She's not a fan.

While we're talking, I'm holding my phone in one hand and rummaging through the freezer with the other. I find a pint of rum raisin ice cream tucked behind a plastic bag of frozen teething rings. "All right if I give Charlie some ice cream?"

"There should be some plain vanilla," she tells me, then asks to speak to Charlie. I aim the phone in my grandson's direction while she waves and coos, "How's my big, big boy?"

Charlie blows tomatoey bubbles and offers his mother a soggy stick of toast. She blows goodbye kisses and hurries off to get dressed for the rehearsal dinner at Spago.

I can't find the vanilla, so I pull my chair up close to Charlie's highchair and dig the rum raisin directly out of the carton. I pick out the raisins for myself and spoon what's left into Charlie. The instant the cold hits his tongue, he grimaces, screws his eyes tight and quivers. Then, his eyes fly open, he smacks his lips and says, "Muh, muh."

"Sure thing, pal," I say and keep shoveling until between the two of us, the carton is empty.

According to my daughter, Charlie has slept straight through the night since he was three months old, so I'm surprised to be awakened a little after eleven by pitiful crying coming through the baby monitor Tansy had installed on the end table next to my bed. As I throw off the covers and pad barefoot down the hall to Charlie's room, I'm thinking maybe all that ice cream after dinner was a bad idea.

I push open the door to Charlie's room. "What's up, little dude?" I begin, but Charlie doesn't say. He's sound asleep, lying spread-eagle on his Elmo sheet. He doesn't even stir when I feel inside his onesie to check his Pampers, which are dry as dust. Maybe a nightmare, I think as I tuck his blankie-bye snugly around him, then wander back to bed.

Around midnight, Charlie awakens me again, wailing. I rush to his room, but whoever's bawling, it isn't Charlie. My grandson's out light the proverbial light, sleeping as soundly as...well, as a baby.

Back in my bedroom, I perch on the edge of the mattress and glare at the baby monitor, a Kinder-Kare V. It's whimpering now, and I hear *shhh-shhh-shhh* and the tinny, tinkly sound of "It's a Small World." Kill me now, I think, as I turn the damn thing off, flop back and burrow under the covers.

The following morning, I relocate the Kinder-Kare V to the kitchen counter while I fix breakfast for Charlie and me. Charlie's deep in concentration, pinching up Cheerios from his highchair tray, closely inspecting each "O" for flaws before conveying it to his mouth. I pop a slice of whole wheat bread into the toaster. "It's picking up signals from somewhere, Charlie," I say as I butter the toast and sprinkle it with cinnamon sugar. I tell him about a woman in Hampton Roads driven nearly mad by Hispanic music playing in her head twenty-four-seven. Turned out she was tuned into AM1050 on her fillings.

"Um," says Charlie.

I slice the toast into strips and hand one to Charlie. I nibble on another strip while I consult my iPhone for the Kinder-Kare V manual I'd Googled online. The units were manufactured in Stuttgart, I learn, and come in eight "playful" colors.

"Eureka!" I tell my grandson after a moment. "The manual says the unit can be tuned to five different frequencies. Some crybaby around here has a monitor tuned to the same frequency as you, but God only knows where," I continue, scrolling quickly down the page, "'cause the damn thing's got a range of anywhere from five hundred to a thousand feet." I take a break to wipe buttery crumbs off Charlie's chin with the tail of his bib. "A thousand feet, Charlie. That's the length of three football fields. Think about it."

Charlie leans forward, not thinking about anything except the slice of banana still left on my plate. I hand it over and continue reading.

According to Professor Google, the fix is super easy—tune to another channel.

I reach for the Kinder-Kare to do just that when a cell phone starts ringing, and I know it's not mine because I'm holding it. Mine wouldn't be playing the theme song from *Titanic*, either. A woman, her voice pitched low, answers without saying hello.

I can't keep doing this, Matt. It's tearing me apart.

Whatever Matt thinks about this remains a mystery. Charlie and I are hearing only her side of the conversation.

I can't live this lie anymore. Every moment with him seems like a betrayal, the woman continues, her voice shaky.

Sometimes I wonder if he suspects anything. If he can see the truth in my eyes.

Then she moans. *It's just getting harder to pretend, to carry on like nothing's happened.*

After a moment, she takes a deep, shuddery breath and says, *Just promise me this will all be worth it.* And then, after a long pause, *I should go before he gets back from the gym. If he hears me...*

I stare at Charlie, and Charlie stares back. "Well, what do you think, pal? Should I fiddle with the frequencies or make popcorn?"

"Pah," Charlie says.

I tip an imaginary hat. "You got it, dude."

* * *

Two days go by before the Kinder-Kare V tunes in on another episode of "As the Lighthouse Turns." Charlie and I'd listened to endless renditions of "It's a Small World" and "Twinkle, Twinkle Little Star" and enjoyed a reading of "Good Night Moon," but he'd already been asleep for two hours, and I was twenty-three-percent into *Shogun* on my Kindle, when the monitor piped up, a man's voice this time.

Hello? Is this, uh, the person I'm supposed to talk to? He's speaking low and gravelly.

Uh, yeah, he says. *Got your number from this guy, Freddy, down at the Bent Cue.*

My wife, uh, she's having an affair, he stammers after a moment, and I'm thinking, poor schmuck, he's got that right. But what he says next makes me sit up straight and drop my Kindle. *She's leaving me and taking the baby. No way that's gonna happen.*

The guy's whispering now, and I'm perched on the edge of the mattress, leaning close to the monitor. Could be talking to an attorney, I reason, but hardly at this late hour, and when he says, *Money's not an issue, man. Whatever it takes, I'll pay.* I know it's serious. I'm wondering what's the going price for a hit job these days. Whatever, they agree on the amount way too quick. *Half now and half when the job's done, okay?*

As I listen in, the husband gives the guy directions to the fitness center on the third floor of the south tower of our complex and explains that his wife works out at ten on Tuesdays and Thursdays when the gym's practically deserted.

Promise me you'll make it look like an accident, he says, and after a couple of beats, he adds, *It's Pilates, man. All those springs, straps, and pulleys. You're a pro; you'll think of something.*

I feel cold, sick to my stomach. I want to curl up in the crib with Charlie and pull his blankie-bye over my head.

Jesus, I can't just PayPal you, ya'know, the husband is grumbling. *Yeah, yeah. I know the place. First thing in the morning. Yeah.*

I don't realize I'm holding my breath until I hear quiet rustling and a whispered, *Sleep tight, Princess.* A door opens and closes. Everything goes quiet.

I gulp in air and reach for my cell phone. My finger's poised over the screen, and then I think, what do I say after the operator answers—*nine-one-one, what is your emergency?*

It's only Thursday, so I wait till the next morning to hash it out with Charlie. I spoon applesauce into his mouth, scrape the excess off his chin, and say, "Who *are* these people, Charlie? Except for that boyfriend, Matt, and some pool hall bum named Freddy, I got no names, nothing. Think about it, kid. A transmitting range of a thousand feet—up, down, and sideways. In this high rise, that other baby's monitor could be just about anywhere.

After breakfast, Charlie and I decide to check out the playground. On weekday mornings, it's usually crawling with kids, their moms sitting watchfully on eco-friendly benches made of recycled soda bottles. I strap Charlie into his stroller, and we take the elevator down to the lobby. I tell Charlie to be on the lookout for a Yummy Mummy with an infant daughter. We walk around for a while, then I buckle Charlie into a bucket swing and give him a push while I survey the playground, acting casual. Merry-go-round, slide, seesaw, climbing rocks all lousy with kids, but none of them young enough to be our "Princess."

Charlie and I are strolling back across the quadrangle when we spot a pretty twenty-something sitting on a bench under a poplar tree, rocking a baby buggy. My spirits lift. When I lean in and make *goo-goo-gah-gah* noises over her daughter, though, she laughs and says, "His name is Michael."

Suddenly, locating our baby's mother seems like mission impossible.

I've been retired for more than five years, but not by choice. Mandatory retirement sucks when you're feeling fit, still in your prime as to knowledge and skills. I decide to handle the situation myself.

On Tuesday morning, early, I tuck what we need into Charlie's diaper bag and park him at Puddle Ducks—the daycare center in the basement of north tower. I cut across the quadrangle to south tower, punch in the access code, and ride the elevator to the third floor. The doors open directly into an expanse of polished wood that gradually gives way to the gleaming tiles that lead to the swimming pool. Water's splashing and the voice of the noodle aerobics instructor is echoing off the ceiling of the solarium—*right arm, left arm, both arms, squeeze, squeeze!*—but the swimming pool is tucked behind a glass cinderblock wall, so I can't see it from here.

To my immediate right, blue foam puzzle mats designate the area where the exercise equipment—treadmills, exercise bikes, rowing and Pilates machines—have been arranged in double rows. Dumbbell racks line the walls beneath floor-to-ceiling windows that offer a panoramic view of the Chesapeake Bay.

A woman encased in pink spandex is working one of the elliptical trainers like an Olympic cross-country skier. With short, tightly-curled gray hair, she seems too old to be the mother of an infant, although with hormones and in vitro, I figure anything is possible these days. I give her a polite nod and step up on a treadmill. Panting, but not missing a beat, she nods back. I've walked about a half mile before the woman steps down, wipes her face with a scrap of towel, and heads for the showers.

I walk another quarter mile before *she* comes in. Instinctively, I know it's her. Not yet thirty, surely, her dark hair is styled in a shaggy pixie cut streaked with purple. She's wearing gray leggings and a racing bra. The only splash of color—other than her hair—comes from a pair of tangerine New

Balance slip-ons. She's carrying a gym bag decorated with Disney princesses. She drops the bag on the floor next to a Pilates machine.

I could stick around, but if I do, the hitman might not show. So, I smile, wave politely, and head for the men's side of the locker room.

I find what I need in the janitor's closet, a neon-yellow tricone with Caution—Wet Floor printed on one side and Cuidado—Piso Mojado on the other. I use it to prop the locker room door open, then move just inside to wait.

Almost right away, I hear a door open. "Mia!" It's the skier, popping out of the ladies.

"Hey, Jan," Mia calls out. "Great timing. Can you help me hook up? I'm starting with my hamstrings today." While Mia lies flat on the sliding carriage of the machine with her neck between the shoulder blocks, Jan stretches the pulleys out one at a time and hooks a strap around each of Mia's feet. Mia's legs start to scissor. The women chat for a while, but too softly for me to hear. Eventually, Jan checks her Apple watch and chirps, "Gotta run. My turn to host book club," and she's gone.

Mia continues to scissor.

I wait.

At ten minutes past the hour, a maintenance worker dressed in dusty blue coveralls shambles into the gym, pushing a broom along a floor already so clean you could eat off it. There's a Lighthouse Towers logo embroidered on his pocket, so he seems legit, until he sweeps past the locker room door and I get a closer look. The trousers are too short, barely covering the top of his socks, which are lime green with a Nike swoosh. The shoes aren't right either—Gucci canvas low-tops? Last time I saw a pair like that was at Neiman Marcus. Priced—on sale—a smidge south of a thousand.

Mia's moved on to working one leg at a time. Her back is to me, left foot resting against a bar and flexing, moving the carriage of the Pilates machine rhythmically out and back, out and back. I hold my breath, watching as the maintenance guy props his broom against the wall and approaches her silently from behind.

Out and back, out and back.

I wait, calculating, praying my timing isn't rusty.

He's looming over Mia like a malevolent vulture when I spring. Muscle memory kicks in as I launch myself out the door and across the floor, closing the space between me and the hitman in seconds. I tackle the guy from behind, knocking his feet out from under him. In four seconds flat, I have his hands behind his back, zip-tied and trussed up like a rodeo calf.

"What the hell...?" he begins, followed by a string of profanity that was breathtaking in its originality.

"Shut up," I say, "Or I'll have to wash your mouth out with soap."

Mia is sitting up on the Pilates machine, eyes wide, hugging herself.

"You got a phone?" I ask.

Tight lipped, silent, she nods and points to her gym bag.

"Call nine-one-one," I tell her, then I turn to the hitman and say, in a voice husky from lack of practice, "You're under arrest. Anything you say can and will be used against you in a court of law..." Yada yada yada, you know the drill. When I yank him to his feet, I recognize the guy, a two-bit thug from Diggs Town who's apparently graduated from vandalism and unlawful possession to murder for hire. You'd think two years in juvie would have straightened the kid out.

Now he's back in custody, singing like a teakettle to my former colleagues in the Norfolk Violent Crimes unit. Mia's husband, whose name is Doug, has a lot of explaining to do, and he's doing it down at the station, too.

My name never comes up, and that's fine by me.

* * *

From his infant seat on the sofa, Charlie uncorks his pacifier and offers it to me, his face solemn.

"Thanks, pal. But I think I need something a bit stronger." I know where Tansy stashes the booze, so I leave Charlie with Peppa Pig on the TV for a few minutes while I fill a glass with crushed ice, top it up with gin and a splash of vermouth, then rummage in the fridge for the olives. I'm stirring my drink with a chopstick from last night's takeaway when I join Charlie again on the sofa. While Peppa Pig attends a birthday party, I take some time to reprogram the Kinder-Kare V, then set it aside. "Now what?" I ask my grandson.

"Bah boo," Charlie begins, but he's cut short by the front door banging open. "Hello, I'm home!"

"I couldn't stand Vegas one…more…minute," my daughter says as she leans over and expertly extracts her son from his carrier. "There was an empty seat on an earlier flight, so I grabbed it," she explains as she folds Charlie into her arms.

She kisses the top of his head. "So, what have you and Grandpa been up to while I've been gone, huh?"

"Not much," I say, grinning. "Watched the game. Knocked back a few beers. Kinda quiet around here, wasn't it, Charlie?"

Comfortably straddling his mother's hip, Charlie grabs a fistful of her hair, skewers me with his baby blues, and agrees, "Gah."

That's my grandson for you. Always has my back.

The Heist

By Bill Pronzini

S omebody was knocking on the bank's rear door.

The sudden noise startled me. Now who could that be? The time was a quarter of four and the Santa Rita branch of Far West Saving & Loan had been closed for forty-five minutes; it was unlikely that a customer would arrive at this late time, and at the rear entrance instead of the front door.

The knocking continued—an odd sort of summons, for it had both an urgent and a hesitant sound, alternately loud and tentative in a sporadic way. I remained where I was, beside the teller's cages in the railed-off section where the branch manager's desk was located. If I ignored the knocking, maybe whoever it was would give up and go away.

No such luck. Judging from the insistence, the person outside knew that the bank was still occupied. It seemed I had no choice but to respond.

I cast an uneasy glance at the carry-all travel bag on the floor beside the desk, then went out through the gate in the rail divider and down the short corridor to the door. The shade was drawn over the glass in the upper half—I had drawn it myself not long ago—so I could not see into the rear parking lot. The knocking, I realized as I reached the door, was coming from down low beneath the glass as if a child were doing it. Frowning, I drew back the edge of the shade and peered out.

The person out there was a man, not a child—a medium-sized, darkly

133

tanned, mustached man dressed in a business suit and tie. He was down on one knee, his right hand stretched out to the door, his left hand pressed against the side of his head. His temple and the tips of his fingers were stained with what appeared to be blood.

He saw me looking out at about the same time I saw him. We blinked at each other. He made an effort to rise, sank back onto his knee again, and said in a pained voice that barely carried through the door, "Accident…took a shortcut through the lot, tripped and fell and hit my head…I need a doctor."

I peered past him. As much of the parking lot as I could see was empty, but the south wall of the bank blocked my view of most of it. I hesitated, but when the man said plaintively, "Please…help me," I reached down reflexively, unlocked the door, and started to pull it open.

The man came upright in one swift motion, drove a shoulder against the door, and crowded inside. The door edge cracked into my forehead; I staggered backward, my vision blurring. When it cleared, and I had my equilibrium again, I was confronted not by one man but by two.

I was also confronted with a short-barreled revolver, held in the hand of the first man.

The second one, who seemed to have materialized out of nowhere, closed and relocked the door. Then he too produced a pistol and pointed it at me. He looked enough like the first man to be his brother— medium-sized, thick mustache, darkly tanned, business suit and tie. The only appreciable difference between them was that the first had long dark hair and the second a bushy blond mane.

I stared at them incredulously. "Who are you? What do you want?"

The dark-haired one said, "Should be obvious who we are and what we want."

"My God," I said, "hold up men."

"Real smart, ain't he?" the blond one said. His voice was scratchy, as if his vocal cords had been sandpapered.

His partner took out a handkerchief and wiped the blood, or whatever the crimson stuff was, off his temple and fingers. Something else was obvious to me then: the two of them wore disguises. The mustaches false, the dark tanning achieved by theatrical makeup, wigs hiding their real hair and color.

"You just do what you're told," the dark-haired one said, "and we'll get along fine." The words were mild, but there was no mistaking the undercurrent of menace in them. "Turn around, walk up the hall."

I obeyed. By the time I stopped again in front of the rail divider, I had regained my composure. I turned once more to face them.

"You're going to be disappointed," I said.

"Yeah?" the blond one said. "What makes you think so?"

"You won't be able to rob this bank."

"Why won't we?"

"Because all the money has been put inside the vault for the weekend," I said, "and I've already set the time locks. They won't release until nine o'clock Monday morning."

The two men exchanged looks. Their faces were expressionless, but their eyes were narrowed and cold. The dark-haired one said to his partner, "Check out the tellers' cages."

The blond nodded and hurried through the divider gate.

The other, clearly the leader of the pair, looked at me again. "What's your name?"

"Robert Winston."

"Your position here?"

"I'm the Santa Rita branch manager."

"You lock up the money this early every Saturday?"

"Yes. As soon as the bank closes at three o'clock."

"How come you don't stay open later than three?"

I gestured at the cramped, old-fashioned room. "We're a small branch bank in a rural community," I said. "We do a limited business; there has been no need for us to expand our hours, especially on Saturday."

"Nobody else in the building now?"

"No. How did you know I was still here?"

"Saw you pull the shade over the rear door window just after we got here. And you didn't leave afterward."

The blond called from inside the second of the two tellers' cages, "Nothing in any of the cash drawers."

The dark-haired leader said to me, "Okay. We'll go back to the vault."

I led the two of them through the gate and down the walkway to the vault door. The leader examined it, tugged on the wheel in a way that told me he had no knowledge of this type of vault, and then turned back to face me. "No way to open this door before Monday morning?"

"None at all."

"You better not be lying about that."

"I'm not," I said. "As I told you, the time locks are set here and on the inner vault door as well. The inner vault is where the bank's assets are kept."

The blond one said, "Damn. I knew we shouldn't of waited so long. Now what do we do?"

The leader ignored him. "How much is in that inner vault?" he asked me. "Round numbers."

"A few thousand, that's all," I said carefully.

"Come on, Winston. How much is in there?"

His voice was still mild, but a sharp waggle of the gun had unmistakable meaning. If I lied to him, the cold eyes boring into mine said, he would do unpleasant things to me.

"Around forty thousand," I told him. "We have no need for more than that on hand at any time. We're—"

"I know, you're a small branch bank in a rural community. All right. How many other people work here?"

"Three. Two tellers and the assistant manager."

"What time do they come in on Monday morning?"

"Nine o'clock. The bank opens at ten."

"Just when the vault locks release."

"Yes, but—"

"Suppose you were to call up those three and tell them to come in at nine-thirty instead of nine. Make up some kind of excuse. They wouldn't question that, would they?"

I realized then what he was getting at. "It won't work," I said.

One of his eyebrows tilted upward. "What won't work?"

"Kidnapping me and holding me hostage for the weekend."

"No? Why not?"

"The assistant manager, if not the tellers, *would* know something was wrong if I asked him to come in late on Monday, no matter what excuse I gave."

"I doubt that."

"Besides," I lied, "I have a wife, three children, and a mother-in-law living in my house. You'd have trouble controlling all of them for an entire weekend."

"So we won't take you to your house. We'll take you somewhere else. You call your family before we leave; tell them you've been called out of town unexpectedly."

"They wouldn't believe it."

"I think they would," he said. "Look, Winston, we don't want to hurt you unless we have to. All we're interested in is that forty thousand."

"That's right," the blond said. "We're a little short of cash right now; we got to have operating capital."

The dark-haired leader told him to shut up. Then, to me, "We'll go out front again now."

A bit numbly I led them away from the vault. When we passed the manager's desk, my eyes went to the leather travel bag beside it and lingered for a couple of seconds.

The leader said, "Hold it right there."

I stopped, half-turning, grimacing when I saw him looking past me at the bag.

He noticed that, too. "Planning a trip somewhere, Winston?"

"Ah...yes," I said. "A trip, yes. To Los Angeles—a bankers' convention. I'm expected there tonight, and if I don't show up, people will know something is wrong—"

"Bull." He glanced at his partner. "Take a look inside that bag."

"Wait," I said. "I—"

"Shut up."

I shut up. The blond one lifted the carry-all to the top of the desk, next to the nameplate there that read *Robert Winston, Branch Manager*. He unzipped it, swung it open.

Surprise dropped his jaw and made him blink. "Hey," he said, "money. It's loaded with *cash*."

The leader stepped away from me and went over to stand beside the other robber, who was rifling through the packets of currency inside the carry-all. Seconds later, the blond said, "What the hell?" and lifted out my .22 caliber Walther P22, which was also in the bag.

Both of them cast dark looks at me. I stared back defiantly. For a little time, it was very quiet in there; then, because there was nothing else to be done, I lowered my gaze and leaned against the divider.

"All right," I said, "the masquerade is over."

The leader said, "Masquerade? What's that supposed to mean, Winston?"

"My name isn't Winston," I said.

"What?"

"The real Robert Winston is locked in the outer vault."

"What?"

"Along with the tellers and the assistant manager."

"What?" The blond said it this time.

"There's close to ten thousand in the case," I said. "I cleaned most of it out of a cash supply in the outer vault before I locked them inside."

"What the hell are you telling us?" the leader said. "That you're—"

"The same thing you are, that's right. A bank robber."

"I don't believe it," he said.

"It's the truth. We seem to have picked the same day to knock over the same bank, only I got here first. I've been casing this branch for nearly a week, though not as carefully as I should have, or I'd have known about the time locks before today. You must not have cased it at all. A spur-of-the-moment heist, am I right?"

"Hell," the blond said, "he is right. We only just—"

"Be quiet," the leader said, "and let me think." He subjected me to a long, searching appraisal. "What's your name?"

"Tom Smith."

"Yeah, sure."

"Look," I said, "I'm not about to give you my right name. Or tell you where I'm from or anything else about me. Why should I? You're not going to tell me your names or give me your resume."

He gestured to his partner. "Frisk him, see if he's carrying any identification."

The blond checked inside the pockets of my suit coat and pants, then ran his hands over my clothing, not gently. "No wallet," he said.

"No ID."

"Of course not," I said. "I'm a pro, same as you are. None of us is stupid enough to carry ID on a job."

The blond returned to where the leader was standing, and they held a whispered conference, giving me sidewise glances all the while. After two minutes of this, they stared at me again.

"Let's get this straight," the leader said. "When did you come in here?"

"Just before the bank closed at three."

"And then what?"

"I waited ten minutes until I was the last person in the place except for Winston and others. Then I threw down on them with the Walther. The inner vault was already time-locked, so I had to settle for what I could get from the outer vault and the tellers' drawers."

"That took you more than half an hour, huh?"

"I spent some time talking to Winston about the time locks. Then, after I locked him and the others in the outer vault, I went through his desk and the assistant manager's to make sure there wasn't any stray cash in them. I was about ready to leave when you showed up." I smiled ruefully. "It was a damned foolish move on my part, going to the rear door without taking my gun with me. But I was afraid it might be the law knocking. And then you caught me off guard with that accident ploy. Pretty clever."

"Good thing you didn't bring the gun along," the blond said. "You'd be dead now if you had."

"Or one or both of you would be."

We exchanged more silent stares.

"Anyhow," I said at length, "I thought I could bluff you into leaving by pretending to be Winston and telling you about the time locks. But then you started that kidnapping business. I didn't want you to take me out of here because it meant leaving the bag, and if you did kidnap me, and I was forced to tell you the truth, you'd dump me somewhere and come back for the money yourselves. Now you've got it anyway—the game's up."

"That's for sure," the leader said.

I cleared my throat. "Tell you what," I said. "I'll split the ten thousand with you, one-third for each of us. That way, we all come out of this with something."

"I've got a better idea."

I knew what was coming, but I said, "Which is?"

"We take the whole ten G's."

"Now, wait a minute—"

"We've got the guns, and that means we make the rules. You're out of luck, Smith, or whatever your name is. You may have gotten here first, but we got here at the right time."

"Honor among thieves," I said. "Hah."

The blond laughed nastily.

"All right, you're taking all the money. What about me?"

"What about you?"

"Do I get to walk out of here in one piece?"

"Well, we ain't going to shoot you. Or call the cops on you."

"You did us sort of a favor," the leader said, "taking care of the details before we got here. So we'll do you one. Tie you up in one of these chairs, tight enough to keep you here while we disappear. You're on your own when you work yourself loose."

"Why can't I just leave when you do?"

That got me a faint smile. "Because you might get a bright idea to follow us and try to take the money back. We wouldn't like that. Neither would you."

I said resignedly, "Some heist this turned out to be."

They tied me up in the chair behind the desk, using my necktie and my belt to bind my hands and feet. As soon as they were done, the leader put my

Walther into the carry-all bag, and without another word, the two of them went out through the rear door.

It took me almost twenty minutes to work my hands loose. When they were free I leaned over to untie my feet and stood up wearily to work the kinks out of my arms and legs. Then I sat down again, pulled the phone over, tapped out a number.

A familiar voice said, "Police Chief Dixon speaking."

"This is Robert Winston," I said. "You'd better get over to the bank right away, Henry. I've just been held up."

* * *

Chief Henry Dixon was a short, stocky man in his late fifties, a competent if not particularly imaginative law officer. I had known him for more than twenty years. While his two subordinates, Fred Conley and Marty Gottlieb—the sum total of Santa Rita's police force—hurried in and out, making radio calls and looking for fingerprints or clues or whatever, Dixon listened to my account of what had taken place with the two robbers. When I finished, he leaned back in the customer's chair across the desk from me and shook his balding head.

"Bob," he said, "you always did have more gall than any man in the county. But this business takes the cake for pure nerve."

"Am I to take that as a compliment, Henry?"

"Sure. Don't get your back up."

"Well, the fact is, I had little choice. It was either pretend to be a bank robber myself or spend the weekend at the mercy of those two men. And have them steal all the bank's funds from the vault on Monday morning—approximately fifty thousand dollars, not forty thousand as I told them."

"Lucky thing you had your P22," Dixon said. "That was probably the clincher."

"That, and the fact that I wasn't carrying my wallet. I was in such a hurry this morning that I left it home on my dresser."

"How'd you happen to bring the gun with you?"

"It has been jamming on me in target practice lately," I said. "I intended to drop it off at Frank Simmons' gunsmith shop tonight for repairs."

"How'd you know those two hadn't cased the bank beforehand?"

"Simple deduction. If they had cased it, they would have known I was the branch manager, and my ruse wouldn't have worked."

Dixon shook his head again, admiringly.

I said, "Do you suppose you'll be able to catch the two of them?"

"Oh, we'll get them, all right. Or the FBI will."

"I hope you're right," I said. I massaged my temples, grimacing a little.

"Headache, Bob? No surprise after what you just went through."

I nodded gingerly. "I had better begin making an exact count of how much money they got away with. The main branch in Sacramento is closed today, but I'll call them first thing Monday morning and have them send an auditor over."

Dixon got to his feet. "We'll leave you to it, then." He gathered Fred Conley and Marty Gottlieb, then paused to grin at me before they left. "Yes sir," he said, "more gall—and more luck—than any man in this county."

* * *

After they were gone, I went to the restroom for a cup of water and swallowed three aspirin. Despite the headache, I felt vastly relieved. Fate, for once, had chosen to smile on me; I had, indeed, been lucky.

But for more reasons than Dixon thought.

Back at my desk, I considered his assurance that the robbers would be apprehended. No doubt they would be, as inept as they were, but not before they spent the money in the carry-all and committed another robbery. I had helped make sure of that by neglecting to mention in my descriptions of them that they'd been wearing disguises.

I had altered my story in a number of other ways. I told Dixon that they got some cash from the vault because the time lock on the door had not yet been activated, which was true, but that they hadn't gotten the bulk of the bank's funds, which were locked in a separate compartment. What wasn't true was that there were not inner and outer vaults; there was only a single vault, and they hadn't realized the door was temporarily hand-locked when they examined it. I said they had carried away the cash in a bag they'd brought with them and that they had discovered the Walther in my overcoat pocket. And, of course, I omitted mention of the fact that I'd deliberately called their attention to the travel case.

I had also lied about the reasons I was not carrying my wallet and why I had the Walther with me. The truth was that I left the wallet at home and put the gun into the carry-all because of a half-formed notion that tonight I would attempt to hold up a business establishment or two somewhere in the next county. I would almost certainly *not* have gone through with that scheme, but I had got myself into a desperate situation. The bank examiners were due on Monday, a month earlier than usual for their annual audit—another fact I'd neglected to tell Dixon—and I had not been able to replace all of the $17,000 I'd "borrowed" during the past ten months to support my regrettable penchant for buying hot-tip stocks on margin that turned out to be worthless.

I had, however, managed on short notice to raise $9,400 by selling my car and disposing of a few moderately valuable personal belongings. The very same $9,400 that had been in the carry-all and that I'd been about to put back into the bank's cash supply when the two robbers arrived.

As things had turned out, I no longer needed to worry about replacing the money or about the bank examiners discovering my temporary embezzlement. Of course, I'd learned my lesson. Under no circumstances would I press my luck by "borrowing" any more of the bank's funds.

I relaxed while I waited for my headache to ease. Since I had done my "borrowing" from the cash supply over a period of time and without falsifying bank records, I had nothing to worry about from the examiners' audit on Monday. For I would tell them, as I would tell Dixon and the FBI, the literal truth.

"The exact amount of the heist," I would say, "is $17,000."

Contributing Authors

Lori Armstrong is the *USA Today* and *Wall Street Journal* best-selling author and two-time Shamus Award-winning author of *Snow Blind* in the Julie Collins mystery series, and *No Mercy*, in the Mercy Gunderson series. Her short story "No Place for a Dame" (*Edgar & Shamus Go Golden*) received a Shamus Award nomination. She has won the WILLA Cather Literary Award for *Hallowed Ground* and was a finalist for the books *Shallow Grave, No Mercy,* and *Merciless. Shallow Grave* was nominated for a High Plains Book Award. Lori is also a *New York Times* best-selling author and *USA Today* best-selling author of contemporary, western, and erotic romances under the name Lorelei James. She lives in western South Dakota.

Libby Cudmore is the author of *Negative Girl (Datura 2024) and The Big Rewind* (William Morrow 2016), as well as the Martin Wade PI series in *Tough, Alfred Hitchcock Mystery Magazine* and *Ellery Queen Mystery Magazine.* Her work has also been published in *Shotgun Honey, Reckon Review, Smokelong Quarterly, Had, The Dark, MonkeyBicycle,* and others. She is a four-year alumna of the Barrelhouse Writer Camp, the recipient of the 2023 Black Orchid Novella Award and Shamus Award, as well as the 2018 Oregon Writer's Colony prize.

John M. Floyd is the author of more than a thousand short stories in publications like *Alfred Hitchcock's Mystery Magazine, Ellery Queen's Mystery Magazine, Strand Magazine, The Saturday Evening Post, Best American Mystery Stories, Edgar & Shamus Go Golden,* and *Best Mystery Stories of the Year.* A former Air Force captain and IBM systems engineer, John is an Edgar Award finalist, a Shamus Award winner, a five-time Derringer Award winner, a three-time Pushcart Prize nominee, and the author of nine books. He is also the 2018 recipient of the Short Mystery Fiction Society's Lifetime Achievement Award.

Carolina Garcia-Aguilera is the Cuba-born, Miami Beach-based, award-winning author of ten books, including the Shamus Award-winning novel *Havana Heat*. Her short story "The Pearl of Antilles" (*Edgar & Shamus Go Golden*) received a Shamus Award nomination. Garcia-Aguilera is also a contributor to numerous anthologies, but is perhaps best known for her Lupe Solano series. Her books have been translated into twelve languages, and a film was made from *One Hot Summer*, her seventh book. Garcia-Aguilera became a private investigator—a profession she has practiced for thirty-five years—in order to credibly write novels and short stories featuring a P.I. as a protagonist.

Marcia Muller has written many novels, short stories, essays, and works of criticism. A *New York Times* best-selling author, she has won six Anthony Awards and a Shamus Award and is also the recipient of the Private Eye Writers of America's Lifetime Achievement Award, as well as the Mystery Writers of America Grand Master Award (their highest accolade). She lives in Sonoma County, California, with her husband and frequent collaborator, mystery writer Bill Pronzini. Her final novel in the long-running Sharon McCone series, *Circle in the Water,* was published on April 23, 2024

Bill Pronzini A full-time professional writer since 1969, Mr. Pronzini has published 90 novels, including seven in collaboration with his wife, Marcia Muller, and 46 in his popular "Nameless Detective" series. He is also the author of four nonfiction books, 23 collections of short stories, and scores of uncollected articles, essays, and book reviews, and he has edited or coedited numerous anthologies. His work has been translated into nineteen languages and published in nearly thirty countries. In 2008, he was named Mystery Writers of America Grand Master, the organization's highest award. He has received six nominations for MWA's Edgar Allan Poe award, as well as three Shamus Awards, two for best novel, and the Lifetime Achievement Award (presented in 1987) from the Private Eye Writers of America. His suspense novel, *Snowbound,* was the recipient of the Grand Prix de la Litterature Policiere as the best crime novel published in France in 1988. Two other suspense novels, *A Wasteland of Strangers* and *The Crimes of Jordan Wise,* were nominated for the Hammett Prize for best crime novels of 1997 and 2006, respectively, by the International Crime Writers Association. He is also the recipient of the Paul A. Witty Award presented by the International Reading Association for the best YA short fiction of 1999, "Christmas Gifts," and of a Western Writers of America Spur Award for best western short fiction of 2007, the novella "Crucifixion River" in collaboration with Marcia Muller. A collection of his best mystery and suspense stories appears in *Cream of the Crop* (Stark House, 2024).

Verena Rose is the co-owner, chief financial officer, and acquisitions editor for Level Best Books and as their representative, Verena is a member of the Crime Writers Association (CWA), and the Crime Readers Association (CRA). While she loves all mystery subgenres, she has a preferred fondness for historical mysteries. In addition to her other duties at Level Best Books, she hosts a podcast, *Sunday Tea with V at the Hystery Chronicles.* She is also the Anthony Award-winning co-editor of *Malice Domestic 14: Mystery Most Edible* and has co-edited numerous other short story anthologies, many of which include stories she has written. Verena is also a member of Mystery Writers of America (MWA), Sisters in Crime-National and Chessie Chapter, and the Historical Novel Society.

John Shepphird is a Shamus Award-winning author, two-time Anthony Award finalist, and writer/director of television films. Novels include *Deception Specialist, Bottom Feeders,* and *The Shill Trilogy.* John's short fiction has appeared in *Alfred Hitchcock Mystery Magazine, Down & Out: The Magazine, Crimestalker Casebook,* and various crime fiction anthologies. He also serves as Chair of the Shamus Awards for the Private Eye Writers of America. As a movie director, his titles include *Jersey Shore Shark Attack,*

Chupacabra Terror, I Saw Mommy Kissing Santa Claus, and *Teenage Bonnie and Klepto Clyde.* Check out *johnshepphird.com*

Shawn Reilly Simmons is an Agatha and Anthony Award-winning author and editor. She's written eight novels in her Red Carpet Catering mystery series, and over twenty-five of her short stories have appeared in various anthologies. She is co-owner of Level Best Books and serves on the Bouchercon board of directors. Shawn is a member of Sisters in Crime, Mystery Writers of America, the Crime Writers' Association, and International Thriller Writers. She also hosts a podcast, Five Compelling Questions with Shawn, where she talks with writers about writing. Shawn lives in historic downtown Frederick, Maryland.

Marcia Talley is the Agatha and Anthony award-winning author of twenty mystery novels featuring Maryland sleuth Hannah Ives. Titles include *Circles of Death, Disco Dead,* and *Done Gone.* She is the editor/author of two collaborative serial novels, *Naked Came the Phoenix,* and *I'd Kill for That,* set in a health spa and an exclusive gated community, respectively. Her short stories appear in more than a dozen collections and have been reprinted in many best-of-the-year crime story anthologies. Marcia is past-president of Sisters in Crime, Inc. and currently serves on the National Board of Mystery Writers of America. She divides her time between Annapolis, MD, and a quaint, Loyalist-style cottage on Elbow Cay in the Bahamas. www.marciatalley.com Twitter: marciatalleybks

About the Editors

Gay Toltl Kinman serves as president of the Private Eye Writers of America (PWA) and has nine award nominations for her writing. She has published several short stories in American and British magazines and numerous anthologies, including *Coast to Coast Private Eyes*, Michael Connelly's *Murder in Vegas,* children's books, a Y.A. Gothic novel, adult mysteries, and other collections of short stories. Several of her short plays were produced—now in a collection of twenty plays, *The Play's the Thing.* Ms. Kinman has published many articles in professional journals, newspapers, and books, including Mystery Writers of America's (MWA) *How to Write a Mystery,* and has co-edited two non-fiction books. For the PWA's Shamus Awards, Ms. Kinman has served as a judge on all the committees, then chair of each. She also served as the overall Chair of the Shamus Awards for many years. For the MWA Edgar Awards, she has served as a judge for the Best Young Adult mystery committee, then chair of the Best Juvenile Mystery, and the presenter to the winner of that category at the annual Awards Banquet. Ms. Kinman has library and law degrees and had the honor of interviewing literary luminaries such as Sara Paretsky, Marcia Muller, and Joseph Wambaugh. She also co-edited *Agatha & Derringer Get Cozy* and *Edgar & Shamus Go Golden,* which was nominated for three Shamus Awards and an Agatha Award.

Andrew McAleer is the author of the *101 Habits of Highly Successful Novelists, Mystery Writing in a Nutshell* (with Edgar winner John McAleer), co-editor of the *Coast-to-Coast* mystery series, *Edgar & Shamus Go Golden,* and *Agatha & Derringer Get Cozy.* Short stories edited by him won the Derringer and Macavity, appeared in the Best American Mystery Stories, and received multiple Agatha, Shamus, and Anthony Award nominations. Author of *A*

Casebook of Crime, a collection of British classic mysteries featuring private detective Henry von Stray (Level Best Books), he also taught classic crime fiction at Boston College and served in Afghanistan as a U.S. Army Historian before returning to public service in the criminal justice system. He is a member of the Private Eye Writers of America, The Speckled Band of Boston, The Friends of Irene Adler, and president of the Henry von Stray literary society—the Benevolent Walnuts. Instagram: mcaleermysteries or henryvonstray

About the Shamus & Anthony Mystery Excellence Awards

The Shamus Awardhas been awarded annually since 1982 by the Private Eye Writers of America (PWA) to recognize outstanding achievement in private eye fiction.

The Anthony Award is a mystery writers' literary award presented at the Bouchercon World Mystery Convention since 1986 and is named after mystery writer and one of the founders of the Mystery Writers of America, Anthony Boucher.

www.ingramcontent.com/pod-product-compliance
Lightning Source LLC
Chambersburg PA
CBHW050451110726
47899CB00003B/892